The Enchanted Bluebell

THE Flower Shop SERIES

International Bestselling Author

McKenzie Rae

The Enchanted Bluebell

The Enchanted Bluebell

To anyone who has a creepy little soul but feels the need to read a happy story now and then.

This one is for you.

The Enchanted Bluebell

Chapter One

Ninette Labelle should not be a dragon's name. It's too posh, too concerned with beauty to belong to such a beastly creature. Yet that *is* my name, and I *am* a dragon. More specifically, I'm a dragon who's in trouble. I really shouldn't have sought shelter in an underground subway station.

"Steady! Hold her down!"

A dozen agents from Creature Control grapple with my neck, wings, and tail. I growl and bare my teeth at the men and one woman who are trying to pin me to the platform. Those are the best places for them to grab my body in order to subdue me safely. If they go anywhere near my legs, I can use my long, sharp claws to rake through their flesh like soft butter. Unfortunately, the Creature Control agents appear to be well aware of this. Dragons are rare enough that, when they cornered me in the

The Enchanted Bluebell

subway station, I thought maybe their training wouldn't be up to date.

Turns out, I'm wrong.

One of the agents puts his knee behind one of my horns, right where my jaw meets my neck. I choke a little and growl at him. Roughly translated, that growl means, "Hey, Neanderthal! You're hurting me." But very few people are well versed in the language of dragons anymore, so to these guys, a threatening growl and a distressed one likely sound identical. In response to my objection about the placement of that imbecile's knee, I get six glorified cattle prods pointed at me.

It's not the rudest way I've ever been told to shut up, but it's certainly the most physically threatening.

"I think we've got a good grip on her," says one of the agents who is keeping my tail immobile. "We're ready for the tranq."

The Enchanted Bluebell

Tranquilizer? I don't remember seeing any of the agents carrying a tranquilizer gun.

But sure enough, from the corner of my eye, I see an agent step forward with a large gun held steady in his hands. The agents pinning my body to the platform all work together to roll me to the side so that the man with the gun has a clean shot at my belly where my scales are thinnest.

Okay, new plan.

Instead of continuing to struggle against my captors, I continue to turn in the direction that they've rolled my body, toward the edge of the platform. I have to ignore the way my right wing *screams* in pain as I force it to bend at an unnatural angle. There aren't many bones in the leathery membranes of my wings, but there are a few, and I have no idea if I've just broken any of them.

Taking the agents by surprise, I successfully break out of their grasp. I roll over a couple of them

The Enchanted Bluebell

that are on the right side of my body. Lucky for them, I'm not a very big dragon. I'm about an inch shy of six feet long, and last I knew, I weigh roughly one-hundred-seventy pounds. So I'm not light by any means, but considering dragons can grow to be fifteen to eighteen feet long, I'd say these guys should be counting their lucky stars that I'm a runt.

I fall four feet from the platform to the tracks below. The Creature Control agents shout to each other. Their words are an indecipherable jumble, and my head is pounding too hard to untangle their meaning at the moment.

I stand up hesitantly, testing my legs. They seem fine, uninjured despite all the roughhousing. Gently, I lean forward and place the fingers that emerge from the tips of my wings on the gravel. A spasm of pain jolts from the fingers in my right wing, running all the way up to my shoulder. Okay, I definitely did some damage there. Wincing, I limp and hop to the other side of the tracks. Behind me, I

The Enchanted Bluebell

hear the agents leaping off of the platform in pursuit. I growl out a curse. If only I was a quadrupedal dragon rather than a bipedal one. My body just isn't built for walking. I'd take being able to breathe fire at this point, too. It's a shame that I've never been able to figure out how to do that.

Given how awkwardly I'm moving, it's hardly surprising that I don't make it to the opposite platform before I'm tackled yet again.

One of the agents speaks into his radio. "This is Agent Frank Lamberti from the Department of Creature Control. We've got an obstruction on the tracks at the Rapunzel Station."

Some of the agents are angry and others are shaken after my brief escape, causing them to be more aggressive than they were before. One of them manhandles my injured wing with little care and sticks his electric prod into my side. I flinch and howl. Another agent, cussing me out under his breath, comes closer to my left leg than he should.

The Enchanted Bluebell

Seizing the opportunity, I lift my leg and gouge my claws into his thigh. He screams and falls to the ground bleeding.

"Watch it!" Agent Lamberti reprimands them. "Agent Sanders, the tranq!"

The only female agent in the group pounces on my back. I squirm, resisting, although I don't see the tranquilizer gun or an electric prod in her grip. Too late, I realize that she has taken only the dart from the gun and clenched it in her fist. Agent Sanders wraps her arms around my neck and sticks the end of the dart between the soft scales under my chin.

Quickly, the subway station swims in my field of vision and fades to black.

***

The Enchanted Bluebell

Reality returns to me one sense at a time. Hearing comes first. Two voices are speaking, arguing with each other. I don't recognize either of them.

Touch comes back next. My belly rests on a cold concrete floor. Cuffs made of a thick, coarse fabric shackle my legs together and connect to a metal chain that I hear rattle with every move I make. Presumably, the chain is attached to either the floor or the wall. I can also feel that my right wing has been secured to my flank by some sort of sling that is strapped tightly around my body.

I take a deep breath and smell a nauseating combination of mildew, feces, and metal. Opening my eyes, I am unsurprised to see the inside of a cage. If I had to guess, I'd say I'm imprisoned in the depths of a Creature Control shelter.

I yawn, still somewhat under the influence of the sedative, and grimace at the sour taste in my mouth.

The Enchanted Bluebell

"Please stop trying to talk me out of my decision when I've already presented you with the proper paperwork," says a woman, her voice growing nearer.

"Yes, ma'am," replies a man who sounds quite frustrated. These are the arguing voices I've heard, only now they seem intent on carrying their disagreement in *my* direction. Their footsteps become louder until both people round the corner and stop in front of my cage.

A young woman with ebony skin stands before me. Her black hair is curly and *big*. It's a textured halo surrounding her determined face. She plants her hands on her hips and assesses me. "This is the dragon from the news?" the woman asks the man, who comes to stand beside her.

He's dressed in a black and gold Creature Control uniform and looks harried, like he's been debating with this woman for much longer than I've been conscious. "Yes, ma'am," he sighs. "That's her.

The Enchanted Bluebell

Female and approximately thirty years old by our estimation."

The woman raises her brows and turns her head to look him in the eye. "Thirty? But she's so small."

Annoyed, I harrumph. As if I'd *want* to be the size of a whale shark—and yet, the tone of her voice still stings. It's like she's finished her assessment and found me lacking.

"Yes, she's small, but our estimate is based on several factors," the agent explains. "We looked at the state of her teeth and her scales, as well as the growth of her horns." He points at the horns atop my head. "The condition of all these is consistent with a female dragon that's roughly thirty years of age."

"Well, if you're sure…" The woman returns her attention to me. Her dark eyes narrow when she notices the sling. "What happened to her wing?"

The Enchanted Bluebell

"She has a hairline fracture in her radial bone and a strained tendon. Nothing to worry about as long as the sling stays on for the next eight weeks."

"Good to know, but that's not what I asked. I want to know how she acquired those injuries."

The agent looks abashed at his deflection being caught and called out. His reaction makes me think he might be one of the agents who subdued me in the subway station, although I don't recall seeing his face specifically.

"She didn't come quietly when she was detained," he admits. The woman clenches her teeth, sharpening the line of her jaw.

"Right." She folds her arms and taps her fingers against the sleeve of her jacket. "If that's all, then I think I'm ready for you to process those release forms."

"Yes, ma'am," he repeats for the third time. The second the agent is gone, the woman's

The Enchanted Bluebell

countenance changes dramatically. Her face brightens with an unreserved smile.

"Hi," she says to me softly. "My name is Tawny, and I'm going to get you out of here."

Chapter Two

True to her word, Tawny nags everyone at the Creature Control shelter whenever it seems like my release is being unnecessarily delayed. Two hours after meeting her, Tawny has secured my conditional freedom, which under the circumstances, is better than nothing.

I'm free to leave the shelter under Tawny's care as long as I don't venture into public without her. The rest of the time, I am to live in the castle belonging to Tawny's grandmother. Before leaving the shelter, she actually asks me if this is what I want. Given the only other option for me is to return to my cage, I quickly bob my head to assure her that I approve of everything she's doing.

If I wasn't worried that the guttural language of dragons would frighten her, I would ask Tawny why she's doing all this. The Creature Control agents

The Enchanted Bluebell

haven't made it easy for her to gain custody of me. If I were in her position, I don't think I would bother.

The two of us exit the building—me with a collar around my neck, and Tawny with a remote that will electrify the collar if activated. I follow her as she begins to walk northbound down the sidewalk. Immediately, I draw the unwanted attention of strangers: humans, elves, fairies, ogres—no one is comfortable with a dragon roaming the streets. I haven't even been free for five minutes, and I'm sure that Creature Control is already being inundated with a plethora of calls reporting me.

I keep my eyes trained on the back of Tawny's figure. She's dressed in jeans and a soft-looking, well-worn blue jacket. Her curls bounce to her energetic gait. She glances at me over her shoulder.

"You're a tough lady to track down, you know that?"

The Enchanted Bluebell

"Is that so?" I reply, which comes out as a gravelly rumble from deep in my chest. It's a short noise, just testing the waters to see if the sound spooks her. Tawny merely smiles. Not the reaction I expect.

"Sorry, I don't speak dragon. But my ward Sasha might. He's a shapeshifter, and I've been informed by a reliable source that they soak up languages like a sponge soaks up scrying water. Speaking of Sasha," she continues, "he also lives at my grandma's castle, so you'll meet him when we get home. Obviously, my grandma lives there too, as well as my brother and a wizard. I hope you don't mind."

A wizard? They're almost as rare as dragons these days. Is Tawny some sort of collector?

"I'm not really in a position to care," I grumble.

The Enchanted Bluebell

Just then, one of my claws catches on a crack in the sidewalk and nearly sends me sprawling. My body isn't made for walking at such a quick pace. Plus, my right wing is in a sling, so I only have one good wing that I can use for balance. Tawny stops and puts her hands on my chest, trying to steady me.

"Sorry." She smiles, sheepish. "I forgot that your range of motion is hampered. I'll slow down. So anyway, we've got a full house at the castle. We could use someone like you, though. I can't tell you too much about it until we get home, but the second I heard about you on the news, I knew you would be perfect for the job! I've spent the last two days just trying to pin down where you were going during your dramatic flight from Creature Control."

I let out a haughty huff, even though Tawny's voice doesn't actually sound judgmental. What does she know about being on the wrong side of Creature Control? I wasn't even doing anything wrong when those guys jumped me. I was just minding my own

The Enchanted Bluebell

business in Goldilocks Park when somebody decided that I was being a public menace.

We pause at a crosswalk, and I take the opportunity to rest, sitting down and carefully curling my tail around my leg. Tawny looks up at me. I can't tell if the expression on her face is one of sympathy or pity.

"For the record," she says, "I think Creature Control overreacted."

The defensiveness I felt seconds ago leaves me, exhaled from my lungs like a cloud of smoke. Those are the nicest words anyone has said to me in a long time.

Wherever it is that Tawny's grandmother lives, we have to board a subway train to get there. I nervously navigate the steps as the two of us enter the underground station. It isn't the same station where I was captured hours earlier, but it makes me anxious nonetheless. Unlike the station from this

*** The Enchanted Bluebell ***

morning, where people were warned and evacuated, this station is busy and crowded. I am surrounded by wary stares and frightened whispers. The only thing good about being bigger than most people is that everyone gets out of my way. Everyone except for Tawny, who doesn't appear to notice the reactions I elicit in others.

It's more of the same when the two of us board a train. I find a spot where I'm mostly not in danger of tripping anybody. Tawny stands by me and smiles pleasantly at anyone who side-eyes us.

We're in the Grimm neighborhood when Tawny ushers me off the train. My legs shake with every step I take. I'm not used to walking so much, and it doesn't help that the effects of the sedative are still lingering. Thankfully, Tawny promises that we don't have much farther to go. The Grimm borough is loud and dirty, smelling strongly of smoke and fish. Despite the fact that some of the fish definitely doesn't smell fresh, my traitorous stomach rumbles.

The Enchanted Bluebell

"My brother should have dinner ready by the time we get home," Tawny tells me. "He knows you're coming, so hopefully he got enough food for everyone. Even if he didn't, we'll figure something out."

I'm seriously dragging my feet by the time Tawny turns down a street filled with Chinese vendors. The scent of fish here is *much* fresher. It makes my mouth water. I draw just as many stares here as I do everywhere else in the city, only I can't tell if these looks are fearful or reverent. Dragons used to be held in high esteem in China. These are Chinese Americans, though—some of them probably second or third generation—so who knows what they think of me.

Tawny leads me to a door situated between a stall that smells tantalizingly of fish sauce and a storefront where the vendor is selling some kind of beef and noodle soup that I'd like nothing more than

The Enchanted Bluebell

to devour. She picks up a brass knocker attached to the door and bangs it against the wood.

"It's Tawny at the Grimm Chinatown entrance!" she yells at whoever is inside.

From beyond the door, I hear a man distantly shout, "Cam! The Chinatown door!"

"I'll get it in a minute!" comes the response. It sounds like the second speaker is even farther away from us than the first.

"I'll get it! I'll get it!" says a third person with a brash enthusiasm that only children possess. Suddenly, the door is thrown wide open, creating a breeze that ruffles Tawny's hair. In the entryway is a boy who can't be older than twelve. His bronze skin is smooth and unblemished by puberty, and the mop of black hair on his head looks like it has an unruly personality of its own.

The boy launches himself at Tawny, his zealous embrace knocking her sideways. She laughs

The Enchanted Bluebell

and pats the back of his head. Then the boy grabs her hand and drags her inside.

"Guys, Tawny's back! And she's got the dragon with her!"

For a split second, I sit in front of the open door, uncertain what I should do. Tawny looks over her shoulder and gestures for me to follow them. Folding my good wing against my flank, I duck inside. Belatedly, I realize that, without a human-sized hand, closing the door will be difficult.

As if a ghost has read my mind, the door swings shut all on its own. Well, that's a convenient enchantment.

I'm now presented with the unique challenge of climbing a narrow staircase without swinging my tail hard enough that I accidentally put a hole in the wall. Miraculously, I make it to the top of the stairs without incident. Although, my dignity is a little

The Enchanted Bluebell

bruised at the way I have to waddle up the steps. Thankfully, no one sees that.

Pausing to catch my breath, I raise my head to take in this castle that Tawny has told me about. The sight I'm met with is an array of flowers, embroidery, and knitting supplies. They cover *everything* in the room. It's nothing to write home about: just a small sitting area filled with furniture that looks like it came from a thrift store. The fireplace is massive, I'll say that much, but it's caked in soot. An abundance of dust motes float through the air, making my nostrils twitch.

This isn't a castle. This is a hole-in-the-wall that hasn't been cleaned in eons.

My stomach chooses that moment to complain loudly and nudges me in the direction of the wonderful aromas wafting from what must be the kitchen. Longingly, I sigh.

The Enchanted Bluebell

Okay, maybe I can plan my escape after dinner.

Chapter Three

I follow my nose to a long, narrow kitchen where all of the inhabitants of this so-called castle have gathered. Tawny is helping a man set the table. Except for having much shorter hair than Tawny, the two look so much alike that I assume this must be her brother. A petite elderly woman with dark skin, curly white hair, and an affable smile is already seated at the table, watching Tawny and her brother bicker about where to place the platters of food.

The boy that answered the door runs circles around Tawny, asking if they can eat yet. Lastly, a pale man with dark purple hair that gradually fades to a light orange enters the kitchen and leans against the wall by a stone oven. He takes in the scene with striking silver eyes.

As soon as she sees me, Tawny calls for quiet. "Everyone, this is the dragon I told you about."

The Enchanted Bluebell

She then addresses the boy. "Sasha, do you speak dragon?"

He shrugs. "I haven't had much practice, but yeah."

To me, she says, "Could you tell Sasha your name?"

My name? I haven't used my name in what feels like forever. Not that I've forgotten it, of course, but it's strange and foreign on my tongue when I utter "Ninette" aloud. Sasha wrinkles his nose.

"She says it's, uh...Nina, I think? Or something like that."

Nina. It's not exactly right, but it's close enough. I kind of like the sound of Nina. It sounds much more befitting of a dragon than Ninette. I bob my head in confirmation. Pleased, Tawny claps her hands.

The Enchanted Bluebell

"Welcome, Nina! This is my grandmother," she motions to the elderly lady, who raises one wrinkled hand in greeting, "Josephine Bellerose. She retired from being a fairy godmother five years ago. And this is my brother Elliot."

She points to the man who has been arguing with her, then gestures to the young boy.

"Sasha Ward, former ward of the state and a shapeshifter. And last but not least is our resident wizard Cam Holmwood."

The purple-haired wizard leaning against the wall is the only one who doesn't acknowledge me in any way. He seems much more interested in picking at his cuticles.

"So," Tawny continues cheerfully, "now that introductions have been made, we can all dig in. After dinner, Nina, I'll give you the grand tour of Bellerose Castle."

The Enchanted Bluebell

I make an attempt at smiling, which comes out a lot more threatening than I intend judging by the veiled fear I glimpse in Elliot's brown eyes. Foregoing the human-sized—and therefore ill-fitting—chairs, I resign myself to an awkward meal seated on the floor.

***

After everyone has finished eating, Tawny takes me on the promised tour. The two of us walk through corridors lit by glowing orbs floating near the ceiling. It turns out that Bellerose Castle is bigger than I initially thought, although no less drab. Even the hallways are dusty and cluttered.

"Most of the castle exists in liminal space," Tawny explains. "Space between worlds, so to speak. That space connects to all of our real-world locations. You saw the entrance in Grimm

The Enchanted Bluebell

Chinatown. Many rooms in the castle are only used for storage these days, so I'll just show you the places you're likely to frequent."

She escorts me to the three suites belonging to herself, Elliot, and Josephine. Sasha's bedroom is down another hallway near the castle's library. When we come to a third passage that appears to stretch endlessly into darkness, Tawny stops and points.

"Cam's suite is down that way. He likes his privacy, so we try not to enter his quarters if we don't have to."

Next, we arrive at a stone archway. A staircase spirals downward. "The dungeon is down there," Tawny says. "That's where you'll be working starting tomorrow."

Curiously, she doesn't take me down to the dungeon to show me around my future workplace. Instead, Tawny takes me to an ascending stairway

The Enchanted Bluebell

and walks slowly enough for my awkward legs to keep pace.

"Your room is up here, Nina. As well as Grandma's greenhouse and Elliot's office. And here's the bathroom..." She opens the bathroom door.

As expected, there is a toilet, a sink, and a tub inside the room. However, these amenities are seemingly set in the middle of a jungle. Thick tree trunks jut up from the floor, draping giant leaves and vines over the shower curtain. Blue and green will-o'-the-wisps dart here and there among exotic flowers. In the distance, I hear foreign birdcalls.

Beside me, Tawny sighs. "Elliot!" she shouts over her shoulder. "The portal under the sink is active again!"

My eye is drawn to the cupboard under the sink where I see a glowing white light that shines through the cracks around the door.

The Enchanted Bluebell

"Cam!" Elliot yells to the wizard.

Cam shouts his reply, "I'll get to it when I get to it!"

"The bathroom doesn't usually look like this," Tawny assures me. "Just, ah...gird your loins when using the toilet."

I eye the jungle bathroom warily as Tawny shuts the door.

Once the tour has concluded, Tawny leaves me in what is to be my bedroom. It's nothing special given the connotations of the word *castle*. My room is attached to the greenhouse. I think it's technically just meant to provide rooftop access to the building, but someone has put two futon mattresses next to each other to act as a bed. The walls are strung with fairy lights, and decorative curtains have been hung strategically to add color to the old bricks and to give me a bit of privacy from the greenhouse windows.

The Enchanted Bluebell

Eyeing the futon mattresses, blankets and pillows piled on top of them, I suddenly find it difficult to keep my eyes open. Futon mattresses have never looked so appealing.

This isn't so bad, I decide as I settle down on my bed. It's possible that my first impression of this place was colored by weariness and hunger. Maybe I won't need to escape from Bellerose Castle after all.

Mere minutes after settling down on my new bed, I'm fast asleep.

***

When I wake, I'm met with a close-up view of Josephine Bellerose's wrinkled face. I snort in surprise and flare my nostrils. Belatedly, I realize that the old woman has one hand pressed flat against my side.

The Enchanted Bluebell

"You're awfully warm for a dragon," she muses in a quiet, raspy voice. Josephine straightens her posture. She's dressed in a floral-patterned nightgown and green slippers shaped like frogs.

"Theoretically, I can breathe fire," I mumble and then yawn. "Why wouldn't I be warm?"

The old woman grins in bemusement. "Reptiles are cold-blooded. I thought you might want a heater for your room, but I can feel heat radiating from your scales."

Cold-blooded, huh? It's never occurred to me that I should need to bask in sunlight or press my belly to a heating pad to regulate my body temperature. I shift under Josephine's gaze. She doesn't appear critical of me, more like she knows more than she ought to know. I grunt and scowl at her, hoping to scare her out of my room. That only serves to widen her grin though, enhancing the crow's feet at the corners of her eyes.

The Enchanted Bluebell

"Well, since you don't need a heater, I suppose I'll just say goodnight." She blows me a kiss, which hits me right between the eyes. I wrinkle my nose at the tickly sensation.

"Witch," I mutter the insult and use my left wingtip to scratch at my snout.

"Nighty night, Nina!" Josephine sings as she leaves my room. She flaps her bony hand in my direction and then turns off the lights in the greenhouse.

Chapter Four

I wake up the next morning to pain radiating from my broken wing. It's still snug in the sling, but whatever pain relievers I was given by Creature Control have worn off. I feel stiff and slightly nauseous when I stand and climb out of my bed.

Dragging my feet through the greenhouse, I take my time trudging down the stairs. I smell bacon coming from the kitchen, which rekindles my appetite. Gritting my teeth against the pain in my wing, I follow the enticing aroma. When I enter the kitchen, I find that every resident except for Josephine is already in attendance. Elliot is standing by the stone oven tending the fire and frying massive amounts of bacon. Sasha is at his side, bouncing up and down, getting as close to the spitting, crackling pan as he can until Elliot pushes him away. At the table are Tawny and Cam. Tawny is dressed and

The Enchanted Bluebell

looks ready for the day ahead. In contrast, Cam is wearing a blue housecoat over flannel pajamas, and his purple and orange hair doesn't look like it's been combed yet. The wizard sips what smells like herbal tea from a porcelain cup, keeping his eyes trained on the open book in front of him.

"Come on, Cam." The way Tawny smiles at him is hopeful and wheedling. "This is supposed to make your life easier. All you have to do is give her some training, and then you'll have more time to focus on your other responsibilities."

Cam drinks from his mug and flips a page. "Babysitting a dragon wasn't in my job description."

His voice is smooth yet somehow grumpy at the same time. He seems immune to Tawny's charm.

"You don't do half the things that *are* in your job description," Elliot comments. He smacks Sasha's hand as the boy tries to sneak a piece of bacon straight out of the pan.

The Enchanted Bluebell

"Precisely my point," Cam retorts, unruffled.

Tawny fixes the wizard with a stern look. "I brought Nina here to help *you* specifically."

"I didn't ask you to do that."

"It doesn't have to be overly complicated," she insists. "Just get her set up this morning. After that, I'm sure Nina will work just fine on her own." It's then that my talons scrape against the stone floor as I shuffle into the room. All eyes turn to me, and Tawny's smile broadens. "Good morning, Nina! You're just in time for breakfast."

"We have plenty of bacon," adds Elliot. "Which would cook a lot faster if a certain wizard would use his magic to help me."

"I'm not the castle chef," Cam peevishly replies. His silver eyes narrow, although he doesn't raise them from the pages of his book.

The Enchanted Bluebell

"Neither am I," says Elliot with a hint of resentment. "But if you'd agree to train Nina to do your work in the dungeon, then you could focus more on other tasks like—oh, I don't know—closing the portal in the bathroom or ensuring that the castle has heat."

The wizard must not have an adequate retort, since he busies his mouth by drinking more tea. Tawny's smile becomes strained as she claps her hands together.

"Well then, it's settled. Cam will spend the rest of the morning training Nina in the dungeon and then start assisting Elliot in managing the castle."

A displeased noise comes from Cam's throat, though I can't make out any intelligible words. Elliot looks skeptical of his sister's suggestion. "I don't know how much help you think he'll be. He's the laziest wizard I've ever met."

The Enchanted Bluebell

In Elliot's distraction, Sasha successfully steals two slices of piping-hot bacon from the pan. The heat doesn't appear to bother the boy.

"He's the *only* wizard you've ever met," Tawny reminds her brother.

"I can train Nina!" Sasha's offer is spoken past a mouthful of half-chewed bacon. I eye the young shapeshifter dubiously. What can I possibly learn from a child?

Tawny shakes her head. "Not now, Sasha. I need to drop you off at school before I go to work. Speaking of which…" Her gaze moves to the large clock mounted on the wall above the doorway to the sitting room. "It's about time to head out. Sasha, you've had more than your fair share of bacon. Let's go!"

Sasha wipes greasy fingers on his jeans. Then he waves to me. "Bye, Nina!"

The Enchanted Bluebell

"Have a good day, everyone!" There's a hopeful gleam in Tawny's brown eyes.

Once Sasha's arms are through the straps of his backpack and his shoes are laced, the two exit through the Grimm Chinatown door.

A steaming plate heaping with bacon is set on the table in front of me. Elliot removes one of the chairs, leaving me room to sit. "Better eat up before Cam finishes his tea and disappears on you."

Cam hums unhappily in response but doesn't let his eyes stray from his book.

I scratch at the collar that is still fastened around my neck as I sit on the floor and greedily snap up four pieces of bacon at once.

***

The Enchanted Bluebell

Despite Elliot's warning, Cam manages to down the rest of his tea long before I'm done eating. By the time I'm done, Elliot has retreated upstairs to his office, and Cam has slunk quietly into the deep shadows of Bellerose Castle.

I stand up from the floor gingerly, trying not to jostle my broken wing. I could search the whole castle for Cam, *or* I could just sniff him out. I raise my snout and test the air. Magic has a peculiar scent. It's difficult to describe. Sort of floral with a bit of citrus—but underneath all of that is a kind of musky odor. I follow the scent to where it's strongest: the entrance to the dungeon. Given how reluctant Cam was to take me under his wing, I doubt he's down there waiting for me.

The next scent trail leads me to the corridor outside Cam's suite. He must be in one of his rooms.

I do my best to lumber along, grimacing every time I jostle my broken wing. The darkness down this hallway is a palpable thing. It seems to

The Enchanted Bluebell

shiver as I pass through it. There's barely enough light coming from the passage behind me to show me the way forward. Up ahead, I see that the corridor veers sharply to the left. Upon rounding the corner, I see a light about two yards away.

It's the hallway I just came from, I realize. Turning back, I retrace my steps only to be met with the same sight. This corridor must be enchanted. Presumably, Cam cast a spell that turns the passage into a loop. No unwanted visitors allowed.

"You shouldn't be here."

At the sound of the wizard's voice right behind me, I whirl around. He has to jump back to avoid the swipe of my tail. In my hurry, I accidentally bump my sling against the wall. "Hasn't anyone warned you not to sneak up on dragons?" I growl at him through clenched teeth. "You might get barbecued."

The Enchanted Bluebell

Cam scowls at me, his silver eyes glowing slightly in the dim light. "I don't understand a word you're saying." He sighs and runs a hand over his face. "Come along, I guess. I'll show you the dungeon."

As Cam takes the lead, I see that he has changed out of his flannel pajamas. He's dressed in dark-wash jeans and an emerald green sweater.

It's a good thing I recall where the dungeon is from Tawny's tour yesterday. The pain from my wing is slowing me down, and Cam is disinclined to slow his pace for me. Eventually, I make it to the descending stone steps and carefully tread the narrow, spiral stairway. When I reach the bottom, Cam is waiting on the landing, impatiently tapping his foot.

Bellerose Castle may not exactly fit my idea of a classic castle, but the dungeon meets my expectations to a tee. It's cold, dark, and dank. The entrance to the dungeon exudes an air of foreboding,

The Enchanted Bluebell

and it reeks of magic down here. We stand in a hallway that's a bit wider than the corridors upstairs, lit only by one glowing orb floating near the ceiling.

Cam nods his head, motioning for me to follow him.

"This dungeon doesn't serve its original purpose anymore, but it is still good for one thing." Cam's voice reverberates off of the stone walls. It echoes along with the sounds of our footfalls.

I can tell that we're coming upon another, larger room. A bluish light is guiding us out of the darkness. I pass through an archway after Cam, who steps aside so I can see the source of the light.

The two of us are surrounded by empty cells situated in a ring around the perimeter of the circular room. In the center of the room is a wooden table that supports a glass box. Inside the box is a single flower that floats in the air. A bluebell.

The Enchanted Bluebell

My jaw drops, for I know this particular flower. I just never believed I would see it again.

Chapter Five

Ten Years Ago

I stand in my new red satin dress in the golden ballroom of the governor's palace. I've only ever seen photographs of this place. It's been a dream of mine to dance across the shiny floor underneath the diamond-studded chandeliers. This event isn't a dance, but I suppose it will do.

The enchanted bluebell is displayed above a crystal bowl filled with water. Besides the fact that the flower is floating, apparently not suspended by wires, there's nothing magical about its appearance. I fold my arms, feeling the smooth satin of my dress caress the exposed length of my arms.

The Enchanted Bluebell

"Big deal," I murmur. "Even *I* could cast a simple levitation spell on a tiny flower, and I've only taken rudimentary magic courses."

My friend, Amalia Farro, comes to stand next to me. "You don't think it's genuine?" she asks in a soft voice.

I roll my eyes, a very unladylike gesture, but my mother and stepfather aren't around to see it. "Of course it isn't," I say none too quietly. "Most of these artifacts are probably replicas."

Amalia and I dressed in our finest clothes this morning to attend the exhibit of magical artifacts being held at the governor's palace today. We took great care to curl and style our hair and to apply our makeup. Unfortunately, the event has been a complete waste of my time. I thought for sure that someone from the royal family would be in attendance. The prince or one of his sisters—perhaps even the queen herself. This is, after all, the first time in seventy-five years that so many magical items have been in the same country at the same time. To my disappointment though, I haven't seen a single crowned head in the governor's ballroom since we arrived.

Not even the governor appears to be here, and he's the host.

The exhibits themselves have been underwhelming to say the least. Everything on display is behind lines of red rope and presented with signs that say *Do Not Touch*. I was certain that someone would be here to demonstrate what each artifact does, but no.

Amalia tucks an errant, brown curl behind her ear. "Why would they be replicas?" she wonders.

"Why *wouldn't* they be?" I scoff. "There's no one to demonstrate their power for us because they're all fake."

"Or because they're dangerous..." Amalia counters with some hesitation.

The Enchanted Bluebell

"If they're so dangerous, then why put all these artifacts in the same ballroom with only flimsy velvet ropes to protect us?"

To prove my point, I lift the bottom of my dress and then duck under the nearest red rope.

Amalia gasps. "Ninette Labelle!" she hisses my full name with reproach. "Get back here!"

"I'm just going to touch it," I whisper back.

I glance around the ballroom. It doesn't look like anyone has noticed what I'm doing. Every guest is dressed to the nines; they're only concerned with rubbing elbows with other important people and drinking their champagne. No one is paying any attention to the two girls at the edge of the ballroom. We're not nearly important enough to warrant anyone's concern, having only scored invitations because Amalia's father is one of the governor's numerous advisors.

The Enchanted Bluebell

I turn back to the allegedly enchanted bluebell. It floats above the crystal bowl innocently, its royal blue color highlighted by the beams of sunlight pouring through the tall windows all around the ballroom. I extend my bare hand toward the flower.

The bluebell's petals are smooth and soft under my fingertips.

Suddenly, the ballroom tilts, although no one else appears to notice this phenomenon or be affected by it. My knees buckle. The last thing I see before I hit the floor is Amalia's horrified face.

***

Present Day

The Enchanted Bluebell

It's the same bluebell, I'm sure of it. It looks identical to the one I touched on that fateful day, and the way it floats inside the glass box… All I did was touch the flower's petals, and when I woke up, I was no longer a pretty nineteen-year-old girl. Instead, I've spent the past decade as a big, ugly dragon. All because of one stupid mistake.

I've looked everywhere for this flower, but I've never been able to find it after that exhibit of magical artifacts closed early. Now, the enchanted bluebell is five feet away, mocking me. My first instinct is to blow a ball of fire at the flower and destroy it. Except I don't know how to breathe fire, and the bluebell's destruction might mean that I'm stuck in this form for the rest of my life. My second instinct is to break the glass box and touch the petals again—only I have no proof that touching it a second time will reverse the spell on me. I could become something even worse, like an enchanted teapot or a

The Enchanted Bluebell

painted portrait of myself. At least as a dragon, I have agency.

Cam stands beside me unperturbed.

"All you have to do is observe the box to make sure there are no cracks in the glass," he explains. "Check the surrounding cells for anything abnormal. Do this multiple times a day, the last time being right before you go to bed. That's it. Come get me if you find anything out of the ordinary."

I glare at the flower. In my periphery, I see Cam lean forward to give me a confused look.

"Did you catch all of that?"

"Yes," I grunt, still staring down the blue flower.

The wizard rolls his eyes. "I can't see this language barrier being a problem *at all*," he mutters.

He leaves me down in the dungeon. I know that I'm supposed to go through the routine he

The Enchanted Bluebell

outlined—inspecting the glass box and all of the cells—but all I can bring myself to do is continue glaring at the enchanted bluebell. Such a delicate, flimsy flower has turned my life upside down, and now I'm expected to guard it? I can't. I won't!

I pace back and forth as well as I can with one of my wings in a sling. My thoughts race, fueled by shock and years of pent-up rage. Has the enchanted bluebell been in this dungeon all these years? Is it *meant* to transform innocent—if somewhat arrogant and naïve—young women into beasts? If so, then there must be an expert, someone who knows how the flower works. I can potentially end this decade-long nightmare within the week!

The logical person to ask about the bluebell is Cam Holmwood. For obvious reasons, that avenue of questioning is bound to go nowhere. There's always the retired fairy godmother. Assuming she's home, of course. She wasn't at breakfast. For all I know, Josephine Bellerose left to go on a cruise early this morning.

Absently, I go through the steps of my new job. Once I'm assured that everything is in order, I hurry back to the stairs. The throbbing of my wing is starting to make me nauseous, but I press on.

The kitchen is empty when I get there. I maneuver past the table and chairs and pass under the arch leading to the sitting room. There is Josephine, looking quite comfortable on a padded wicker chair as she works a crochet needle.

"Good morning," the old woman says in her raspy voice. "How goes it guarding the dungeon?" Josephine's eyes flit up, and I see a twinkle in their brown depths.

Annoyed, I flare my nostrils and huff. "That bluebell," I growl. "Do you know what it does?"

The Enchanted Bluebell

Josephine's bony shoulders bounce up and down as she quietly laughs. "Sorry, sweetie, but I don't speak dragon. Though you don't sound happy."

"I've been looking for that magical flower for ten years!" I rant.

I start trying to pace again. One of my talons snags a tassel on the rug, and I stumble, falling straight for the china hutch that's loaded with very breakable tea sets, plates, and glass goblets.

Josephine purses her lips and blows a gust of air in my direction. Magically created in the air is a cushion that forms between my ungainly body and the china hutch, softly breaking my fall and saving the delicate contents of the shelves. The puff of air doesn't stop my wing from being jostled by the movement, though. I growl and shudder at the throbbing pain and attempt to curl around the wounded limb.

The Enchanted Bluebell

Josephine eyes me thoughtfully. She takes her crochet needle, waves the pale rose-colored yarn hanging from it, and flicks her wrist. Rosy smoke rises from the yarn. It floats toward me and darts up my nostrils. My body convulses in a series of sneezes. I glare at Josephine, only to realize a second later that the pain in my broken wing is gone.

Smiling to herself, she nods. "Much better." Then she waves her crochet needle again, this time at the record player in the corner. The needle drops, and a jazzy tune begins to play softly. Josephine pats her knee. "Come keep me company, Nina. I first became a fairy godmother back in a time when that job was still considered 'woman's work,' so I have decades and decades of stories to share. And it's been quite some time since I've had a fresh audience…"

Chapter Six

After I get over my initial shock of seeing the enchanted bluebell again, I find that performing my job isn't difficult at all. It helps that whatever Josephine forced me to inhale has thoroughly numbed my broken wing.

Around one in the afternoon, Elliot makes lunch. He presents a grilled cheese sandwich to his grandmother, three cheeseburgers for me, and a Caesar salad for himself. The only person he doesn't cook for is Cam.

"Cam is welcome to eat lunch with us if he wants," Elliot says. He sets a bowl of water in front of me with more force than necessary, sloshing some of the contents over the side of the bowl. "He never does, though."

I don't see the wizard from the time he leaves me in the dungeon that morning until the time Tawny and Sasha are due home in the early evening. I'm once again resting on the rug in the sitting room while Josephine naps when I hear a knock. It doesn't sound like it comes from the Grimm Chinatown entrance, which is confirmed a couple seconds later by Elliot.

"That's the door in Rose Red Courtyard!" he yells from the kitchen where he's preparing dinner. "Cam!"

"I'm in my potion room!" Cam's voice sounds distant, floating up from the depths of Bellerose Castle. "I'm a little busy!"

I glance at Josephine. She grunts in her sleep, and her nose twitches at all the noise, but she doesn't otherwise stir. With both Elliot and Cam occupied, I guess it's up to me to answer the door. I stand up only to realize that I don't know where the door to Rose Red Courtyard is located. Shuffling into the kitchen, I catch Elliot's eye.

The Enchanted Bluebell

"Go to the library and then hook a right," he tells me. I bob my head and set off to find the Rose Red Courtyard door.

It's easy to locate the library again, and the door in question is just around the corner. True to its name, the door is even painted a rich shade of red. Carefully, I use the tip of my good wing to push down on the handle. The door swings open, permitting Tawny and Sasha to enter.

"Hey, Nina!" Sasha waves to me as he darts around the bulk of my body.

"Thanks for letting us in," says Tawny with a smile. "We lost the keys to the castle last time the portal under the sink was active. Cam's been trying to make a new set, but magical castles notoriously resist change."

My eyes widen. The Bellerose Castle is home to a dangerous, enchanted flower, and they can't even lock or unlock the main doors at will? No

The Enchanted Bluebell

wonder Tawny hired a dragon to beef up security. They need all the help they can get.

***

Dinner that evening is similar to yesterday's fare. Everyone is present, including Cam, who appears exhausted and grouchy. Unlike the previous day, everyone except the wizard retires to the sitting room once they're done eating. There, they exchange stories about how everyone's day went over a foldable card table that Elliot lugs in from a different room. I feel so...*warm* being surrounding by happy people playing cards—or in Sasha's case, doing his homework. My life before *and* after my transformation never felt like this. Cozy and peaceful.

I almost fall asleep on the rug when Tawny gently nudges me awake and urges me to go to bed.

The Enchanted Bluebell

I drag my feet upstairs, through the greenhouse, and into my little bedroom lit by fairy lights. They look like fireflies, I think before my eyelids fall shut, and I drop my heavy head onto the pile of pillows.

My slumber is deep and untroubled for most of the night. When my eyes suddenly pop open, the castle is dark and silent. With a yawn, I sit up on my haunches, wondering what woke me. At first, I can't figure it out. The castle is quiet; the only sounds I hear come from outside, and those are just typical city noises that I've heard all my life. No one is up and moving around, as far as I can tell. Even my fairy lights turned themselves off sometime after I fell asleep.

But then, I feel it. A sense of wrongness. Sniffing the air, I smell magic. Not just any kind of magic, though. The odor of this magic has a sour tinge to it.

Something isn't right.

The Enchanted Bluebell

I roll out of bed, careful of my broken wing, and pad into the greenhouse. Exotic flowers—nonmagical flowers, I hope—fill this space with vibrant colors muted by the darkness. Creeping ivy clings to the windows and climbs the walls. Even through the overwhelming floral scents of the greenhouse, the smell of *bad* magic is still pervasive. My claws scrape against the stone floor as I make my way to the stairwell. Following my nose, I slowly tread down the steps.

The foul odor leads me past the suite of rooms belonging to Tawny, Elliot, and Josephine and then toward the magically darkened corridor that belongs to Cam. As I learned earlier, he has a spell on the hallway to keep people out. However, the corridor isn't as dark as it was this morning. I see more of those glowing orbs floating near the ceiling leading deeper into the castle. Perhaps the enchantment has worn off. The bad magic smell is *definitely* coming from Cam's suite. It would be

The Enchanted Bluebell

irresponsible not to investigate, wouldn't it? Whatever he's doing in his suite could affect the enchanted bluebell, so I'm only doing my duty, not being nosy.

Yeah, that sounds believable.

The scent of bad magic gets stronger the farther down the corridor I go. The floating orbs flicker, casting odd shadows on the walls. Or, maybe those *aren't* shadows...

Cautiously, I nuzzle the tip of my snout against a bulbous shadow that appears to be three-dimensional. I'm right, I realize as the cold stone touches my scales. It isn't a shadow; the walls are misshapen. They bend and buckle, distend in a bloated fashion and jut out sharply in other places. Walking on, the ceiling gradually turns to rough-hewn rock.

It isn't long before I'm traversing a cave rather than a passageway of Bellerose Castle.

The Enchanted Bluebell

Soon, I see a green light that leads me around a corner. A black caldron floats in the middle of the room. Green light shines from it, and a noxious, black smoke overflows from the rim of the caldron. Shelves line the walls of the room. On them are glass vials of potions, packages of dried plants and powders, and plastic containers for wet ingredients. This must be Cam's potion room.

Suddenly, the caldron begins to shake and belches more smoke. Coughing, I stumble backwards. Right into Cam, as it turns out. He howls when I accidentally step on his foot.

"What's the matter with you?!" The wizard's voice jumps up an octave while he hops around on one foot.

"Me?" I retort. "I'm not the one who's brewing shady potions in the middle of the night." Glancing down at his foot, it's impossible to ignore just how much bigger my feet are than his. "I am sorry about your foot, though," I mumble.

The Enchanted Bluebell

Cam stops hopping and limps toward the trembling caldron. "Did you sneak in here when I went to recast my looping spell on the hallway?"

"I wasn't *sneaking*," I grunt defensively. "I smelled bad magic and thought there might have been something wrong with the flower." My lie would be more believable if I'd actually gone to check on the enchanted bluebell, but it's not like Cam has any idea what I'm saying.

He flings his arms out and then draws all of the black smoke to him, wrapping it around the caldron until the bowl stops quaking. His shoulders slump as the green light wanes to a mere glow. "Just my luck," he mutters. "I turn my back for ten seconds, and it's ruined!"

Mindful of where I place my feet, I step closer to look over his shoulder. Cam takes a ladle and dips it into the green potion. He fishes a rustic key out of the caldron. "Is that a new key to the castle?" I wonder aloud.

The Enchanted Bluebell

Frustrated, the wizard flings the key across the room with a shout. "I don't even know how I closed the portal last time it was open! How am I supposed to do it again?" He pulls at his dark hair and paces the room.

Ah, so that key was meant to close the portal under the sink. Then the rest of his words sink in.

"Wait, you don't know how to close the portal?"

Suddenly, his reluctance to do his job seems like it might have less to do with laziness and more to do with insecurity. His haughty attitude that he's worn like a suit of armor is nowhere to be seen at the moment.

He's stressed. He's worried. He's alone.

I stop his frenetic pacing by gently grabbing the collar of his sweater with my teeth. He makes a very undignified noise of surprise, but I shush him by emitting a soothing rumble from deep in my chest.

The Enchanted Bluebell

It's the dragon equivalent of a cat's purr. I hear the fabric of his sweater stretch as I lift his body a few inches off the floor. Cam sounds a bit like he's being strangled. I'm not too worried about him since I'm not taking him far.

I waddle out of the potion room with the harried wizard clasped between my fangs. I carry him until I locate his bedroom, which appears both cave-like and cozy. The walls of his room are plastered with posters of famous wizards and magical artifacts, as well as paintings and three-dimensional pieces of artwork. Colorful trinkets and doodads make the room feel lived in. His small bed is tucked into a corner, pressed against the wall and piled high with quilts and blankets.

He coughs and gasps for air once I set him down. I huff at him. How dramatic.

Taking care not to rip anything, I use my teeth to pull back the blankets on his bed. Then I butt my head against the small of his back. Cam stumbles

The Enchanted Bluebell

toward the bed, glaring at me even as he strips out of his clothes. Feeling heat rise to my cheeks, I turn my back on him and lie on the floor.

A minute later, Cam clears his throat. I glance at him and see that he's dressed in his flannel pajamas. I wonder if he's going to order me to leave now, but instead he just says, "Goodnight, Nina." Then he motions to the glowing orb near the ceiling, and the room grows dark.

Chapter Seven

I wake up early the next morning, mostly because I've been sleeping on a cold, hard floor. Standing up, I stretch my one good wing, crack my neck, and then shuffle out of Cam's bedroom. Nature calls, and the half bath on the first floor is too small for me to comfortably use. To relieve the pressure on my bladder, I have to climb the stairs and go to the bathroom with the portal under the sink.

The corridors are deserted. The only things I hear are the clicks and clacks of my own claws scraping the floor.

As I use my good shoulder to push open the door of the bathroom, I'm greeted by quite the sight.

Last time I was in here, the bathroom appeared to be set in the middle of a tropical jungle. Today, it looks like the bathroom is inside a giant

The Enchanted Bluebell

purple geode. Light bounces off of one wall to another and glides across the glittering ceiling.

Using the toilet is a little tricky, especially when I find that the water in the porcelain bowl has been replaced with magma that bubbles and spits. I'm just pondering whether I should flush given the state the toilet is in, when a loud *bang* rattles the cupboard under the sink.

Startled, I freeze and stare as a blue light begins to shine from the cracks around the cupboard door. My nostrils flare, and my legs tense. Then the cupboard is flung open so forcefully that the hinges pop and groan under the strain. A wall of lucent blue water spews into the room. Quickly, I wade to the bathroom door and work the handle with my mouth.

A wave washes me into the hallway. Sitting on the floor in a soggy heap, I watch the corridor turn into a river.

Elliot is going to be *thrilled* by this.

The Enchanted Bluebell

***

"How did the water tank burst?" Elliot asks the room as he cooks eggs and hash browns with an angry vigor.

Apparently, *that's* where all the water from the portal came from. Since only certain rooms of the castle are physically attached to the city, Bellerose Castle has its own water supply. The castle is currently flooded with any water that we hoped to use for cooking, drinking, or showering. Upon waking up in a shallow pool, Sasha transformed himself into a goldfish. He's been swimming around my ankles all morning.

"The water tank was ancient," Tawny replies. "This was bound to happen eventually." She wrings out rugs and blankets that have been soaked in the

The Enchanted Bluebell

flood. Then she drapes them over anything above the water to let them dry.

Cam sits at his spot at the table, although he's without his usual cup of tea. He has his legs folded above the water and a book in his hands. Glancing at it over his shoulder, I ascertain that it's some sort of academic text. What the subject matter is, I can't tell.

Josephine is seated on the table itself. Her legs are folded like a pretzel, and her eyes are closed while she holds her hands above the rug from the sitting room. Steam rises from the rug as she magically purges water from its fibers.

"Hey, Cam," Elliot says and shoves a giant plate of scrambled eggs and hash browns in my direction. "Can't you just take all this water and put it back?"

From the corner of my eye, I see the wizard raise one brow while maintaining his gaze on the pages of his book. "In theory, that's possible. But the water tank exploded, so…"

"Well, can't you fix the water tank?"

"You mean the one that *exploded*?"

"There's nothing else for it," Tawny chimes in before Elliot and Cam's argument can spiral out of proportion. "We'll have to purchase a new one." Placing her hands on her hips, she turns around to face the rest of the room. "Since it's an emergency, I should be able to move my work hours today. I'll call in and then shop around this morning. Nina, if you and Grandma could walk Sasha to school, I would owe you one. I'd feel more comfortable if Grandma didn't go alone."

"Sure," I agree. "I'll just check on the bluebell before we leave." As I move away from the table, I realize that I have no idea what Tawny does for a living. "Where do you work, anyway?"

The Enchanted Bluebell

Of course, Tawny can't understand me, so she snaps her fingers at the goldfish jumping out of the water attempting to nibble on Cam's bare toes. Sasha transforms back into a boy dressed in swim trunks. Standing up, he shakes the water out of his black curls. "Nina says she'll help take me to school, and she wants to know what your job is," he translates.

"I'm a private alchemy tutor," Tawny replies, beaming with pride. "I have two families that I regularly work for, and thankfully, they're very understanding of my need for a flexible schedule."

She places her hand on Josephine's shoulder, and the retired fairy godmother opens her eyes.

"Here's the remote that controls Nina's collar, Grandma." Tawny takes the small, black device out of her pocket and puts it in the old woman's open palm. "Having the remote on you is the only legal way Nina can leave the castle."

The Enchanted Bluebell

"Yes, yes, yes." Josephine flaps her hand dismissively at her granddaughter as she accepts the remote. "I understand, Tawny."

Before we leave, I hurry down to the dungeon to look in on that accursed blue flower. It remains suspended in its glass case, and all of the cells remain empty. After I return upstairs, I'm swept up in a flurry of wet shoes, backpacks, and splashing feet as the four of us exit the castle and enter Grimm Chinatown.

Tawny opens the door, sending a wave of water flowing into the street. Shouts of surprise and complaints arise at the miniature river that's just been emptied into the road. The nearest vendors, who are setting up their stalls and displaying goods outside their storefronts for the day, glare at us. Tawny cringes at the water that rushes past our feet.

"Sorry," she says to the vendors.

The Enchanted Bluebell

I feel their displeased stares follow the four of us until we round the corner. My large, clawed feet splash in puddles as I waddle down the sidewalk, waving my good wing in the air for balance. On the bright side, whatever magic Josephine worked on me the other day continues to keep the pain in my broken wing at bay.

Tawny walks the four of us to the nearest subway station. Like the last time I was out in public with her, Tawny seems immune to all the glares and stares that come my way. Sasha preens by my side, reveling in the attention. The sea of strangers parts for me when we board a train. As I expect, the gawking only gets worse when we're all packed into a tight, enclosed space together.

Wrapping my tail around my legs, I press my flank against the opposite door. I gaze into the dark glass, trying not to meet anybody's eye while we're all trapped together in this tiny, underground box. Despite my efforts, I still see eyes trained on me in the black reflection of the window. Behind me, I feel Sasha lean against the curve of my spine.

"This is my dragon," he proudly tells a man dressed in a business suit. The man clutches a black briefcase to his chest. "Her name is Nina, and she guards our castle."

In the reflection of the window, I see the man's eyes widen. Then he narrows his gaze on me. "Good for you, young man," he says to Sasha, wrinkling his nose in disapproval.

We spill out of the train after two stops. This is where we part ways. I sit back while Tawny doles out goodbye hugs. I'm a little surprised when she includes me; she wraps her arms around my neck as much as she can, giving me a comforting squeeze. All I can do is sit there and accept the embrace with wide eyes.

Tawny waves farewell until the three of us turn onto a new street and disappear from her sight.

The Enchanted Bluebell

We haven't even made it down the block when Josephine steps under an awning in front of a department store and halts. Concerned that the old woman has already exhausted herself, I snag Sasha's backpack in my teeth and force him to wait. When I turn back to Josephine, she wears a mischievous smile like it's a favored piece of jewelry.

"Well, now that we're alone," she says and rolls up the baggy sleeves of her dress, "let's get this collar off of Nina."

I pull back in shock. "What?" She's not allowed to do that. It was part of the deal that Tawny made to get me out of Creature Control's custody. Sasha apparently doesn't share my concern.

He beams and bounces on the balls of his feet. "Awesome!"

With a flick of Josephine's fingers, I hear a click, and the collar falls from around my neck to the sidewalk.

Chapter Eight

I'm...free.

The collar weighed almost nothing, but its absence leaves me feeling tons lighter. Josephine tosses the remote and the collar into the nearest trash can and then carefully steps over the curb. She motions for me and Sasha to follow her.

"Come along, you two."

"But school's that way." Sasha points down the sidewalk in the direction we'd previously been going.

"It is indeed," Josephine agrees with a secretive grin. "I am going *this* way, though." She shuffles closer to the yellow line between the sidewalk and the busy street.

Sasha raises his eyebrows hopefully. "So...no school today?"

The Enchanted Bluebell

"There will be time for school tomorrow. I, however, am not getting any younger."

With that, the retired fairy godmother steps into traffic.

Tires screech as cars swerve out of the way, and angry drivers honk at her. Crazy witch! What does she think she's doing?

With very little grace, I leap into the road after her. For an old lady, she's quite nimble, darting from lane to lane. For my part, I'm busy trying to keep myself between Josephine and oncoming traffic, acting as a barrier between her and certain death.

I don't immediately notice when my feet touch the curb on the other side of the street. Not until I lift my head and spot Josephine calmly waiting on the sidewalk. I crane my neck, searching for Sasha. He has transformed himself into a brown barn owl. He swoops over the tops of cars, clutching one strap

The Enchanted Bluebell

of his backpack in his talons. Tucking in his wings, the owl dives down, transforming back into a boy just in time for his feet to land lightly on the concrete.

Now that we're all safely on the other side of the road, I round on Josephine.

"Are you insane? You could've killed us! There's a crosswalk just down the block, you loony, old coot!"

Josephine smiles serenely at me. "Sorry, dear, but I don't speak dragon. Remember?"

I growl a string of curses at the woman. She looks at Sasha with expectation written upon her face, making him glance nervously at me.

"Uh...most of that sentence doesn't really translate," he says in a rush, rather than tell her the truth. It's generous to call the tapestry of profanity I just wove a sentence.

The Enchanted Bluebell

Josephine shakes a gnarled finger at me. "Mind your tongue around the boy, Nina." She smirks as she says this, so I'm not sure if I'm being reprimanded or teased.

Faster than it seems possible, Josephine is off again. Sasha runs after her, shifting into a brown, short-haired dog. He's forgotten his backpack this time, so I grab one of the straps between my teeth and bring up the rear of this crazy train. I am *so* getting sent back to Creature Control for this disastrous outing.

I finally catch up to them in front of a store called Happily Ever After Supplies spelled out in looping gold letters. With a flick of her fingers, the door swings open for Josephine, and she ushers us inside.

The scent of the store hits me first: floral and fruity with a hint of beatific magic. The walls are painted a light rose pink, and a crystal chandelier hangs elegantly from the vaulted ceiling. Shelves of

The Enchanted Bluebell

multicolored bottles line the walls, and display tables are sprinkled throughout the store. A sign in the entryway says: *Welcome to the fairy godmother's ultimate supply boutique!*

That explains why there are so many fairy godmothers flying hither and thither. Their delicate, lustrous wings fluttering sound like the whirring blades of a quiet fan. I look from the other fairy godmothers to Josephine and wonder where her wings are. Despite our language barrier, she correctly interprets the meaning of my curious look.

"When I retired, I had to turn in my wings," she explains. Her eyes wistfully follow the employees and other customers zipping around the store. They remind me of oversized hummingbirds.

While Josephine appears nostalgic, Sasha looks like Christmas has arrived early.

"Cool! Magic wands!"

The Enchanted Bluebell

At the sight of Sasha reaching for a display table full of different types of magic wands, memories of the enchanted bluebell flash before my eyes. A sudden panic seizes me, and I'm overcome with a conviction that, under no circumstances, should Sasha be allowed to handle magical objects. In my haste to stop him, my tail makes a wide sweeping motion and collides with a heavy display case made of glass.

I whip around to see the glass case—full of sparkling vials of fairy dust—teeter. A chorus of gasps erupt from nearby patrons, and someone shouts, "Look out!"

Before disaster strikes, I quickly wrap my body around the glass case. It sways a little, but with my body there to stabilize it, the case doesn't tip over. Once it stops moving, I let my muscles relax and ease away from the case of fairy dust. Relief leaves my legs wobbly, but that sense of relief doesn't last long.

The Enchanted Bluebell

"Whose dragon is this?!"

The busy beehive of activity has screeched to a halt. Everyone stares at me in fear and horror. A fairy godmother, with golden blonde curls on her head and a gauzy blue dress swaying around her legs, flies toward me. Her round cheeks are rosy with outrage and one fist is clenched around a glass wand.

"Nina is with me, Ella." Hands on her hips, Josephine approaches the enraged fairy godmother. "And it's perfectly safe for her to be here. She just forgot about her tail for a moment, but she remembered in time to prevent any damage." The old woman smiles. "No harm done!"

Upon seeing Josephine, Ella's blue eyes widen. I can't tell if the sight of Josephine inspires reverence or fear in Ella. Her wings cease fluttering, and her satin slipper-clad feet drop to the floor. "Godmother Bellerose! I'm sorry, I-I didn't know this was *your* dragon."

The Enchanted Bluebell

When Ella next looks at me, her eyes are kinder although no less fearful.

"I guess, as long as she doesn't cause any trouble...she can stay."

Those words look like they've left a foul taste is Ella's mouth. She hurries away from us, motioning for everyone else in the store to go back to what they were doing before I so rudely interrupted their day. Josephine stands by my side, looking rather proud of herself.

"Josephine, you're kind of a big deal around here," I murmur in awe. Who would have thought that tiny, quiet Josephine would have so much fairy godmother clout?

She pats my flank affectionately. "You're welcome, Nina."

When Josephine wanders off, I want to protest being left by myself. I get the feeling that the employees and other customers won't be quite so

The Enchanted Bluebell

nice to me if the retired fairy godmother isn't by my side. I've also lost track of Sasha in all the hubbub. It's probably not a good idea to go looking for him, though. It's best if I just stand here by the wall and move as little as possible until Josephine is ready to go.

That's the plan until I hear someone to my left clear her throat. Looking down, I see a young fairy godmother with flaming red hair and dressed in a daisy-yellow dress. She hesitantly points to the shelves behind me and clears her throat again.

"Um...excuse me."

Ah, right. I'm blocking these shelves.

Furtively looking all around me, I see that people are working so hard to ignore my presence that a lot of them are inadvertently in my way. The only direction I can move is to the right, but then I'll wind up trapped in a tight corner. And the only escape from there will be to squeeze around another

The Enchanted Bluebell

display table of glowing pink potion bottles. This seems like a bad idea, but I can't exactly ask people politely to please clear a path.

Awkwardly, I shuffle out of the redhead's way. I hope that she'll be fast about whatever she needs so that I can get out of this corner without needing to navigate any narrow passages. But apparently, she feels the need to take her time browsing. I try to make myself comfortable in my little corner of the shop. Soon though, my good wing starts to cramp with the unfulfilled need to stretch.

"Hey, Nina!" Sasha yells. "Look at this!"

Tipping my head back, I see the boy on a balcony above me. He leans over the railing and dangles a wishing coin over my head. Taking a big breath, he then blows on the coin, sending a shower of golden sparks flying and sizzling through the air. One of those sparks goes straight up my nostril. Before I can stop myself, a forceful sneeze shakes my

The Enchanted Bluebell

body, and my wing shoots out, knocking over the table of potion bottles.

Chapter Nine

The table tips, bottles crash, and I become enveloped in a cloud of pink smoke. Coughing and flailing, I attempt to move away from the crowded corner before I break anything else. More bottles crack and shatter under my feet. The potions sizzle between my scales, burning the skin underneath them. I don't know what these pink potions are meant to do, but I'm guessing that they shouldn't touch dragon skin based on this itching, burning sensation.

I hop from one foot to the other, searching desperately for an escape route. As the haze of pink smoke begins to dissipate, Ella's enraged face appears. Wings vibrating, she hovers over my head and points her glass wand at me.

"Out, out, out!"

Sparks fly from the tip of the wand, exploding aggressively when they touch my scales.

The Enchanted Bluebell

The explosive sparks are more startling than they are painful—but either way, Ella succeeds in herding me out of the shop. She slams the door on me, leaving me with nothing to do but sit on the sidewalk and scratch at my itchy skin.

A minute later, Sasha surreptitiously slips outside. Before the door swings shut, I hear the sounds of chaos inside the shop. The boy wears an expression of guilt.

"Sorry, Nina. I didn't mean to get you in trouble."

My nostrils flare as I heave a sigh. "I know you didn't."

When he looks up, his brow furrows. "Nina, you're pink!" He wipes a finger over a scale on my chest. His finger comes away clean. "I guess it's not a residue."

"Residue, huh? Big word, little Sasha."

The Enchanted Bluebell

He's right, though. I look down at myself to see that my brown scales have turned a fuchsia pink. I give my body a shake and wipe my feet on the sidewalk. No pink dust falls off of me, nor do I manage to wipe any of it onto the concrete.

The door opens again, and Josephine is gently escorted out of the shop. The old woman is all smiles and mischievous giggles. "Oh, goodness! That was fun. It's things like this that keep me feeling young." Josephine gestures for us to follow her. "Come along, you two. Let's get ice cream."

***

A day of ice cream and window shopping has never been so exhausting. People's stares have an added weight to them now that I'm a *pink* dragon. After several hours, Josephine looks me over and announces, "You're still pink, Nina," with an air of

The Enchanted Bluebell

surprise. As if she'd assumed the effect would wear off with time.

We head back to Bellerose Castle and knock on the door in Rose Red Courtyard. Two minutes pass where all I hear inside is the sound of Elliot and Cam shouting back and forth, arguing who should get the door. Eventually, the door swings inward, revealing a grumpy wizard. Cam looks bedraggled and angry that he's lost his squabble with Elliot. His hair is askew, and he's dressed in a pair of old sweatpants.

Breathing heavily, he looks down at Sasha. "What are you doing here? You're supposed to be in school."

Sasha shrugs and says, "Josephine decided to get us ice cream," and brushes past Cam.

The wizard shakes his head. "Of course she did." That's when he sees me. "Is Nina *pink*?"

The Enchanted Bluebell

Josephine comes up beside him, gazing up at me. "Isn't it strange? Dragons aren't typically affected by magic, and yet, a few spilled potion bottles dyed Nina's scales fuchsia."

There's a knowing twinkle in Josephine's eyes as she slips past Cam and walks into the castle.

Cam somehow appears even more fatigued when he looks at me again. The bags under his silver eyes seem to grow heavier, the tired circles around his eyes grow darker. His whole body sags when he sighs.

"I guess you should follow me, Nina."

I duck through the doorway. Walking behind Cam, I stare at the stooped set of his shoulders. The poor guy is totally drained. I'm guessing that he hasn't had any luck with closing the portal under the bathroom sink or with creating a new key to the castle. I feel bad for the guy.

The Enchanted Bluebell

Pity isn't something I often feel for other people, given the situation I've been ensnared in for the past decade. In a way, though, Cam Holmwood is also trapped. He's a wizard who apparently isn't very confident in his own abilities. He has a job here at Bellerose Castle, but he doesn't feel skilled enough to attend to all of his responsibilities. From a mental and emotional standpoint, that makes it difficult to look for a different job if he doesn't believe he can do the job he has now.

Cam temporarily lifts the looping spell in the corridor outside his suite. The stone walls gradually change to the same cavern-like walls I saw the last time I was here.

The two of us make our way to a wide set of French doors. They open onto a sunlit terrace. I shuffle through the doorway and gaze upon a panoramic view of the city. In the distance, the domed roof of the governor's palace catches the afternoon light and gleams like a golden star.

The Enchanted Bluebell

Wherever this terrace is located in the city, we must be close to a bakery, because the scent of pastries on the breeze is strong. From somewhere outside the castle, I hear the faint strains of a violin and an accordion.

Cam drops like a heavy sack of potatoes onto a patio chair by a round, glass table. He rests his chin in one hand and motions for me to come forward with the other one. "Make yourself comfortable."

The last word transforms into a yawn.

There's no chair large enough to accommodate me, but there is a small pergola on the other side of the terrace. It's wrapped in vines, and there are spheres of soil hanging from the overhead grid. Growing out of the spheres are ordinary bluebell flowers that hang downward, turning in the direction of the sun. Careful not to knock over any of the flowerpots situated on the floor around the pergola, I sit down beneath the delicate bluebells.

The Enchanted Bluebell

I expect Cam to do…*something*. But he just sits at the table. From here, it almost looks like his eyes are closed. Did he fall asleep?

I make a chirping noise at him. A polite reminder that I'm still here. The way his head snaps up, I think he might actually have dozed off. Did he not sleep well last night? I was on his floor, and I slept just fine.

"Right," he mumbles and roughly rubs his palm over his face. "You're pink. You're a dragon, and you've been magically dyed pink."

Hysterical laughter erupts from his mouth.

"I don't know how to fix you! Just like I don't know how to close the portal. I'm useless!"

Cam lets his head fall into his hands.

There was a time not so long ago when I would have cruelly agreed with him. I would have seen his flaws, seen the way he's fallen apart, and dismissed him entirely. As a young woman, human and beautiful, I would have sneered at his pathetic, directionless life. As a woman newly turned dragon, I would have railed at him, in anger and hatred, for having everything that had been stolen from me.

But today, I see Cam defeated and feel a pang of sympathy.

I stand up and shuffle over to him. He doesn't lift his head. I'd think that he's fallen asleep again, except that his back rises and falls too quickly. My wing feels tense as I extend it and gently lay it across Cam's back. This may be the first time in my life that I've attempted to comfort someone other than myself. The act feels foreign and awkward.

Cam's head pops up. He looks first to my wingtip curled around his arm and then looks up to my face.

"There, there," I say, trying not to grimace. With a reticent huff, I force myself to go on. "Listen,

The Enchanted Bluebell

you're not useless. You're just…lost. I know how that feels. I've been lost for *years*. Even now that I've found that enchanted bluebell, I still may never be my old self ever again."

The more I speak, the more Cam's facial expression changes. He goes from looking shocked at the comforting wing around his shoulders to confused—by what, I'm not really sure. Then that confusion morphs into astonishment.

"Nina," he breathes my name. "I *understood* that!"

Chapter Ten

Cam resembles a man revitalized by this sudden revelation. He jumps up from the table and circles me, looking me up and down. From my pink horns to my pink tail. With a broad smile and bright eyes, he desperately waves his hands at me and says, "Say something else!"

I duck my head, suddenly feeling self-conscious for some reason. "Uh, okay...something else."

"Ha!"

Cam and I both jump, although for very different reasons. The wizard begins to furiously pace the terrace, his excitement so great that he can't physically contain it. "What's just happened and how?" he murmurs to himself. "Do I now understand dragon somehow? Or did the potion that dyed her pink affect her speech?"

The Enchanted Bluebell

He turns on his heels and narrows his eyes at me.

"You're not doing anything different when you speak, are you?"

I shake my head.

"And I don't think I suddenly understand the language of dragons," he adds. "I haven't done anything differently that would account for it. Say something again, Nina."

My nostrils flare in irritation. "What am I, a dog? You can't just *command* that I speak."

Confusion eclipses elation on Cam's face. He tilts his head as he stares up at me. "That time, all I heard were growls. What just changed?"

"How should I know?" I mutter. Based on Cam's lack of reaction, I'm guessing he didn't understand that either.

The Enchanted Bluebell

Before Cam and I have the chance to figure this out, a loud *bang* comes from inside the castle. In unison, we both run back indoors. Given that my legs aren't built for running, Cam quickly outstrips me. I follow the sight of Cam's back as I sprint through the dark caverns of his suite. By the time I emerge into one of the main corridors of the castle, I've lost sight of Cam completely.

I hear a commotion upstairs.

The source of the ruckus is in the upstairs hallway right outside the bathroom. Cam and Elliot shout at each other as fireworks explode from the bathroom doorway. The two men are huddled together, clearly fighting.

"You need to close the portal *now*, Cam!"

"If I could, don't you think I would?"

Elliot throws his hands in the air in frustration, only to then cover his head when something in the bathroom explodes. A chunk of

The Enchanted Bluebell

white porcelain flies into the corridor, forcing both Elliot and Cam to duck.

"Just do whatever you did last time!"

I swallow hard, and my eyes dart to the wizard, who's trying not to look guilty. Only Cam and I know that closing the portal under the sink was a fluke the last time it opened. The poor guy refuses to look at me or Elliot when he speaks.

"Elliot, I—"

More fireworks go off and shake the walls. Before Cam can say whatever it is that he wants to say, Elliot catches sight of me. "Nina!" He rushes over to me, almost tripping over his own feet in his eagerness. "You're a dragon!"

"Oh, you finally noticed that?"

What he apparently *hasn't* noticed is that I'm now a pink dragon. But the bathroom is being inundated by colorful explosions, so I'll give him a pass this time.

"You won't be affected by the fire or the magic," he says excitedly and points to the open doorway. "You can go in there! Do something, Nina, please!"

I lean forward and peer into the bathroom.

It's a lightshow in there. The bathroom has remodeled itself again; this time it's in a meadow full of bluebell flowers. The fireworks are shooting out of the portal beneath the sink. A larger explosion erupts from the toilet, taking another chunk out of the bowl. The piece shatters against the opposite wall, showering the floor in shards of broken porcelain. My instinct is to say "See ya!" and run in the opposite direction. But that's not why Tawny brought me—a dragon—here. I'm supposed to face dangers and protect the castle.

The Enchanted Bluebell

In the past, failing someone else's expectations wouldn't have bothered me. Well, it would have, but I would have claimed otherwise. I *have* done that, and I hated myself every single time. Maybe it shouldn't be such a revelation, but I'm only just now realizing that I don't want to disappoint people anymore.

I want to be brave.

I move fast so that I don't have time for second thoughts. Charging headfirst into the chaotic bathroom, I throw my body against the cupboard door under the sink, trying to force it shut. For such a small door that isn't being held open by anything substantially solid, the cupboard door puts up a lot of resistance. My scales grow hot from the searing heat of the fireworks. There's a magical heat in the air as well; I can feel it attempting to warp the curve of my horns and to peel my scales off like scabs.

It seems to take forever to force the cupboard door shut, but in reality, it's only been a minute. Not

The Enchanted Bluebell

that duration makes much of a difference now that my body feels achy and nauseous.

In the absence of explosions, the silence is deafening.

I stand there for a moment, swaying. Just when I think I'm okay, my stomach turns. I have just enough time to hunch over the busted toilet bowl before my last meal makes a reappearance. From the corner of my eye, I see Cam and Elliot cautiously step into the bathroom. When nothing dramatic or dangerous happens, Cam hurries to my side. Gently, he places his hand on my sling.

"Nina, are you okay?"

I take a deep breath. "Yeah, I think so."

A crease appears between his brows. "You shouldn't have been affected like this."

The Enchanted Bluebell

Elliot whirls around from where he's been examining the tub and the showerhead. "Did I just hear Nina *speak*?"

"I've always been able to speak," I snap as I stretch one wingtip out to fiddle with the faucet in the sink. Only after I've managed to turn the knob and nothing happens do I recall that the castle's water tank burst. Great, now I can't wash the taste of vomit out of my mouth.

"You understood her too?" asks Cam.

Elliot nods. "Yeah. Is that *your* doing? I thought dragons were immune to most magic spells." He looks me over then and does a double take. "Why is Nina pink?"

"I don't know, but I think your grandmother had something to do with it."

Not directly, but at least Cam is on the right track.

The Enchanted Bluebell

Well, since these two seem content to talk about me like I'm not here, I might as well make myself scarce. Someone should probably check on the enchanted bluebell after this incident.

I feel lightheaded as I shuffle down one flight of stairs and then another. Nothing in the dungeon looks out of place. The enchanted bluebell doesn't appear harmed; the glass case isn't even cracked. There's a fly buzzing around the box, but I snap it out of the air and swallow it. After that, nothing else in the dungeon moves.

The Enchanted Bluebell

Chapter Eleven

All I've known of Tawny thus far is a kindhearted optimist. However, when she arrives home that evening, she is understandably upset by the day's events. She's heard from the school that Sasha was absent, which then leads Sasha to explain how he spent his day. Tawny's jaw drops. The way she looks between me, Josephine, and Sasha, it seems that she can't decide who she should direct her righteous anger toward. But then she hears about the incident in the bathroom, and suddenly Sasha's truancy and her grandmother's shenanigans take a backseat.

"Fireworks?" Tawny looks her brother up and down, searching for injuries. "The portal's never done that before. Are you okay?"

"Yeah," Elliot assures her. "Nina was the one who put a stop to it."

The Enchanted Bluebell

Tawny turns to me, her expression one of pleasant surprise. It makes me think I might already be forgiven for letting Josephine run loose all over the city.

"Oh! Well, great job, Nina." Her smile broadens. "I knew that you were just what this place needed."

I grunt wordlessly as I settle down at one end of the kitchen table. I still feel a little off ever since I shut the cupboard door in the bathroom earlier today. I'm not sure I'll be able to eat much of whatever Elliot is cooking for dinner. Such a shame since it smells delightfully like seasoned pork.

"I was kind of limited on what I could make since we have no water," Elliot explains apologetically. He sets dishes of food on the table. "Any good news on that front, Tawny?"

"Actually, yes!"

The Enchanted Bluebell

She dives into a more detailed account of her day searching for a new water tank, which I tune out. Lethargy makes my body sag, and my stomach churns. I startle when someone sets a cup on the table in front of me. A light blue liquid swirls inside the glass. Looking up, I see that it's Cam who's offered me this drink. Odd, considering that the wizard usually just sits at the table and ignores everyone while he eats. Right now, he watches me with attentiveness.

"That's a potion meant to restore health," he says. His voice is quiet, so it doesn't draw the attention of Tawny and Elliot, who continue their discussion about the varying prices of water tanks.

"Thanks," I murmur.

"You're welcome," he replies and claims the chair next to me.

Eating and drinking from bowls and cups is tricky. My wingtips don't really have the dexterity to

The Enchanted Bluebell

pick up cups or hold silverware. It means that I'm a bit of a messy eater; it's not something that Cam has ever attempted to aid me with—Tawny or Elliot tend to provide assistance when they notice me struggling. So it's weird that, when he sees me fumbling with the glass, he leans forward and tips the contents into my mouth.

As I swallow the potion, a cool feeling of peace washes over me. The nausea disappears, and the lethargy recedes leaving me feeling perkier. I sit up straight and flex my broken wing that's pinned down by the sling. Though Josephine's spell took the pain away, the limb has still felt fragile. But suddenly, my wing feels strong again.

When he sees me fidgeting and biting at the sling, Cam unclasps the contraption. Able to move freely for the first time since Tawny found me at the Creature Control shelter, I stretch my previously fractured wing. It feels like new, strong and whole.

The Enchanted Bluebell

When the others realize that Cam has removed my sling, they express concern for my injury. But, once it's apparent that my wing is no longer broken, their concern becomes amazement at my sudden recovery. I don't pay them any attention, though. I can't take my eyes off of Cam, who's staring at me not with wonder like the others, but with suspicion.

***

It's incredible how much easier it is to move around the castle with both my wings at my disposal. It leads me on another round of exploration, this time unguided by Tawny or Cam. It's kind of fun now that I'm not in pain or encumbered by a sling. I don't even care that most of the rooms I find are dusty and full of old furniture or boxes of ancient paperwork—old tax filings, by the looks of them.

The Enchanted Bluebell

Outside my bedroom and Josephine's greenhouse, I come upon a long, winding staircase. I follow it all the way to the top of a tower. Exiting the stairwell, I enter a breathtaking observatory. The domed ceiling is made of glass panels so that the massive telescope in the center of the room can offer a clear view of the sky while remaining protected from the elements. The telescope looks like it's sculpted from ice—though maybe that's because the floor appears to have a snowflake design.

Perhaps it's the curved shape of the roof or the way the sky seems magnified by the glass, but the stars—the ones that are just barely visible in the waning light of the sun—look like they're almost within my reach.

"I see you discovered the observatory."

I don't need to look or hear his voice to determine that it's Cam who's found me. There's always a whiff of magic about his person; it trails

The Enchanted Bluebell

after him like a subtle cologne. I hear his footsteps traverse to the telescope.

"I imagine Tawny didn't show you this place because of all the stairs. That, and you really have no need to be up here."

Flaring my nostrils in irritation, I turn to look at him. "Well, I didn't see a sign on the door saying to keep out."

Cam has cleaned himself up, even though it's nearing the end of the day. He has changed out of his sweatpants and into a pair of corduroys, as well as a navy-blue knit sweater. His dark purple and orange hair has been washed and combed. Even those silver eyes of his look sharper, less tired. His gaze shifts from the telescope to me. There's a spirit of inquiry in the way he tilts his head.

"I didn't understand you that time." The heels of Cam's shoes click on the stone floor as he walks closer to me. "What's curiouser is that my healing potion apparently worked on you when it shouldn't have. Same as that mystery potion that dyed you pink."

"Good to know that you healed me out of scientific curiosity," I sneer at him. "Instead of—oh, I don't know—the goodness of your heart."

He comes to a halt only when his nose is mere inches from my chin. When he speaks again, his voice is nearly a whisper.

"You're not a real dragon, are you, Nina."

It's worded as a question, but spoken like a statement.

In all my years of living under this curse, no one has ever put two and two together and confronted me with the correct conclusion. An unexpected knot forms in my throat. I've waited so long for someone to look at me and see past the enchantment that I don't know what to do now that it's finally happened.

The Enchanted Bluebell

"And I assume Josephine has already figured it out. She dropped a not-so-subtle hint pointing out how *strangely* pink you are."

Hm... Now that I think about it, she probably *does* know. She's probably known since she realized that I'm not cold-blooded.

Taking my silence for confirmation, Cam backs away from me and lets loose another one of those hysterical laughs that I heard on the terrace.

"Fantastic! Tawny hires a dragon and somehow manages to find the only dragon impersonator in the city—maybe in the entire country! And Josephine puts the puzzle pieces together but neglects to mention it to anyone." He thrusts an accusing finger at me. "Do you realize that you could have been *killed* walking into that bathroom today?"

"Since when do you care about my safety?" I retort. "You don't even want me here!"

The Enchanted Bluebell

Cam runs frustrated fingers through his hair. "I don't understand you! I can't..."

Breathing heavily, he trails off. He averts his eyes and wipes his nose on the back of his sleeve. After a minute, his breathing slows. Cam speaks again but this time without meeting my gaze.

"You can't help with the portal anymore. And I want you staying out of the dungeon as much as possible while still doing your job. That means you go down there to check on the enchanted bluebell, and then you get out. No lingering."

An angry growl rumbles deep in my chest. "Excuse me? You can't order me around like I'm—"

"Do as I say," he cuts in, "or I'll send you back to Creature Control." Cam shakes his head, dejected. "I'm sorry, Nina, but right now you're just another liability that we don't need."

The Enchanted Bluebell

Those words cut to the quick. An ache makes itself known in my heart, like the muscle is slowly being torn open and left to bleed all over this floor of chiseled snowflakes. I stand motionless and silent while I watch Cam exit the observatory, his head hanging low. As though, somehow, this conversation has hurt him just as much as it hurts me.

Chapter Twelve

I can't stop hearing Cam's voice in my head. It's like the worst song ever is on repeat, and nothing I do will make it stop. It keeps me up that night after everyone else has gone to sleep. Lying on my bed made of futon mattresses, I stare at the ceiling and try to ignore Cam's words from the observatory.

I'm just a liability that no one needs.

All I bring to the table is trouble. People are better off without my presence. That was true before I turned into a dragon, and it's certainly true now. Self-pity suddenly swings, converting to simmering anger. A liability! What makes Cam think I can't do my job now that he knows I'm not a real dragon? I'm still the same non-dragon I was when Tawny brought me to the castle.

Before I've fully realized what I'm doing, I roll out of bed and head for the stairs. Single-minded,

The Enchanted Bluebell

I march on until I'm in the dungeon standing in front of the enchanted bluebell.

The flower hovers in the air, trapped by its glass cage. It does nothing else—it doesn't even rotate in place. What's so hard about watching a flower that never moves? What makes Cam and Tawny think that only a dragon can guard this magical plant?

I sit on the stone floor and stare at the bluebell until my eyes are sore. The longer I sit here, the more my anger and determination slowly fade, as though they're seeping into the cold floor along with my body heat.

Weariness and doubt creep in. What exactly am I trying to prove by pulling a nightshift in the dungeon? That I'm good enough to do a job that I didn't want in the first place? That's stupid.

What do I want?

The Enchanted Bluebell

For years, I've told myself that I want my old life back. But the hard truth is that my mother and stepfather never came looking for me after I disappeared. Every few years, I've peeked in on them, and they constantly have their hands full with my stepsister and half-siblings. Me disappearing—with all of my teenage resentment, jealousy, and angst—actually made their lives easier. If I go back to that life now, I'll not only be re-burdening myself with all of those ugly feelings, but I'll also be taking away the peace my family has found.

So the question remains: What do I want?

Well, I know what I *don't* want. I don't want to be a burden or a liability. I don't want to force myself into the lives of people who don't desire my presence. I don't want strangers staring at me in fear or contempt. I don't want to be chased out of a public park for doing nothing but watching the ducks on the pond.

The Enchanted Bluebell

I suppose I want to be somewhere else. Anywhere else.

I'm not sure what makes me reach for the glass box with my wings. I only really become conscious of what I'm doing when one wingtip slips underneath the case. A noise behind me makes me pause seconds away from touching the flower's stem.

"Nina?"

As I whirl around, the abrupt motion sends the glass case tumbling to the floor where it shatters. In the doorway stands Cam in his flannel pajamas and blue housecoat. His silver eyes glow in the dark and appear to have no trouble taking in the scene. He looks from me to the uncovered bluebell. His eyes widen fearfully.

"Nina, get away from there!"

I look back at the flower just in time to see a tendril of shimmering blue light slither out of the

The Enchanted Bluebell

bluebell's mouth and stretch toward my wingtip. Then, like a viper, it snaps out and grabs me. I feel Cam's hand grip my left wing just as the light from the bluebell explodes.

In an instant, all of the air gets sucked from the dungeon. The light from the bluebell winks out of existence, leaving me in total darkness.

***

I don't know where I am. I've never experienced this kind of absolute darkness, where the lack of light is tangible. Turning around, I face a pair of luminous eyes staring back at me.

"Ah!"

"Nina! Nina, it's me!"

The eyes sound a lot like Cam Holmwood. I hear him snap his fingers, and the glow from his

The Enchanted Bluebell

silver eyes brightens, illuminating our immediate surroundings. We're in a cavern, on the edge of a subterranean pool. The light from his eyes doesn't radiate outward far enough to show me how big the cavern is or where an exit might be located.

"How did we get here?" I gasp.

"The enchanted bluebell," Cam replies. "The real question is *where* are we, and how are we going to get out?"

My head snaps back to confront him. "You understood me?"

He cocks his head. "Yes. Can't *you* hear the difference between when you're speaking dragon and when you aren't?"

"I..." I start to say that all I hear is the guttural dialect of dragons when I realize that that isn't entirely true. Just now, I heard English words when I spoke. "I guess I wasn't paying attention until now."

The Enchanted Bluebell

"I take it that you've never involuntarily switched from one oral language to another?"

"Not that I've noticed."

Although, our chats are some of the longest conversations I've had since my transformation. It's possible that I've had the ability to speak English all along; I just haven't had anyone to talk to in the past decade.

"Fascinating." He studies me with a look that's somewhere between awe and scientific inquisitiveness. "You're clearly not a shapeshifter, so what were you prior to posing as a dragon?"

"Human. Until I encountered that bluebell."

In the dark, I nearly forget what he said to me hours ago. Then it occurs to me how odd it is that we're having this completely normal discussion when, the last time he and I talked, he stuck a metaphorical dagger in my heart. Averting my eyes

The Enchanted Bluebell

with a huff, I look down at the placid, glass-like surface of the pool.

"Let's just find a way out of here," I mutter. "And then I'll leave your precious bluebell alone. You have my word."

I start shuffling toward the edge of the water when Cam's hand shoots out to gently grab my wing. My feet stop moving, but I don't turn to face him. "You switched again," he says. "From English to dragon. Was that intentional or…"

Now that I pause to think about it, I see that he's right. I *did* switch, but it wasn't a conscious effort. I've always thought in English, but usually when I speak, my words come out in growls and rumbles. I open my mouth and try to make my tongue form English words. However, as soon as I actively attempt to recreate this phenomenon that Cam's discovered, I feel a hitch in my tongue. The stutter is so bad that I can't say anything at all.

The Enchanted Bluebell

Frustrated, I let out a huffy growl. "I *can't* do it if I'm thinking about it."

Cam shakes his head. "That was dragon again. Could you tell?"

I can now that he points it out, but just like every time previously, I can't tell which language I'm speaking in the moment. It's only after the fact that I can make the distinction. Scowling at him and flaring my nostrils, I say, "Can we figure this out later? We're kind of in the middle of a crisis."

Just by looking at Cam's face, I know that I'm still speaking dragon.

Turning my back to the wizard once more, I dip my toes into the pool. It's wet and cool against the pads of my toes. It *feels* like ordinary water, but I'm not making any assumptions. Using the silver light emanating from Cam's eyes, I search the narrow shoreline for something to throw into the pool. The only thing that fits the bill are some small

The Enchanted Bluebell

stones. I kick one of them into the water. With a splash, it sinks quickly to the bottom. It's hard to see, but nothing awful or unusual appears to have happened to the stone.

Deciding to take a risk, I wade into the pool and dive below the surface.

The water is even darker than the rest of the cavern. I can't see where the deepest part of the pool is or tell how far down I'll have to swim to reach it. One of the perks of being a dragon is the lung capacity; this pool would have to be pretty deep to keep me from finding the bottom. Sure enough, my toes touch gravel and sand about thirty seconds later. I swim around the floor of the pool until I'm certain that there's no way out down here.

I resurface to find Cam sitting cross-legged on the shore, pointing his glowing eyes toward the water. I could be wrong, but it looks like he was attempting to create a sort of floodlight for me to see by under the water.

The Enchanted Bluebell

"Anything down there?" he asks.

Unsure whether English or grunts and growls will come forth if I open my mouth, I simply shake my head as I trudge out of the water. Cam's reaction to this is calm acceptance.

"Well, then. I guess we should prepare ourselves to be here for a while."

Chapter Thirteen

It's infuriating how cool-headed Cam is being about this situation. Just a few hours ago, he was a hot mess, and now that we're in a real emergency, he's the picture of calm. He hasn't moved from his spot on the gravelly shore; meanwhile, I've been swimming in the pool, gliding around the ceiling of the cavern, and pacing the shore in frustration when neither of those activities provides us with an escape. All the while, he just watches me and points his glowing eyes wherever he thinks I may need light.

It's impossible to tell how much times has passed, but eventually I wear myself out. I collapse in a wet heap on the shore several feet away from Cam. Once it becomes clear that I'm done running around our prison, he speaks up.

The Enchanted Bluebell

"I've been thinking about something you said, Nina."

"Just because we're stuck together," I growl at him, "doesn't mean we have to talk."

I pause to consider what I've just said and note that it wasn't in English. Cam doesn't point it out this time. He just continues along his train of thought.

"You said you were human until you encountered the bluebell." The glow from his eyes brightens as he turns his head toward me. "You meant the enchanted bluebell in the dungeon, didn't you?"

Well, I certainly wasn't talking about the flowers on the terrace. Aloud, I merely grunt in response, which he takes as a yes.

"You've had contact with it before. I wondered... Before the bluebell dropped us here,

The Enchanted Bluebell

when it reached out, it almost seemed like it *remembered* you."

I shoot him a look that is unamused. That's interesting, I suppose, but it doesn't help us in our current predicament.

With a sigh, Cam gazes up at the stalactites hanging from the ceiling. "Sorry that I'm not doing more to help you find a way out of here," he murmurs. "It's just that…being stuck here…it's kind of a relief."

I tilt my head at him and frown. He presses his lips into a humorless smile.

"I can't close the portal from here. I can't do *any* of my normal duties from this cave. I've finally found a place where Elliot's and Tawny's expectations can't reach me."

I sit up straight and stare at him, dumbfounded. "You *want* to be trapped in this cave?"

The Enchanted Bluebell

"I didn't understand you that time," he admits, "but I'm guessing that you think I'm a coward."

There's a spiteful part of me that wants to agree with him. It wouldn't be true, though. It would only be cruel to allow Cam to believe one of his worst fears about himself. Even though my voice is quiet when I open my mouth, it still echoes throughout the cavern.

"I don't think that."

Cam looks at me again, this time with surprise and a hint of hope in his eyes. I'm going to go out on a limb and assume that I've switched back to speaking English.

"If you're having a hard time," I continue, "why don't you talk to Tawny about it? She seems like the kind of person that would understand, that would try to help you. That's the only reason she went looking for me, isn't it?"

The Enchanted Bluebell

"You're probably right," he says softly. "I just...don't like the thought of disappointing her. I don't want Tawny to look at me and think that she made a mistake by hiring me."

With a sympathetic sigh, I move closer to him. "Yeah, I know the feeling." I take a deep breath and swallow hard. "What you said to me in the observatory hit pretty close to home. Even before I turned into a dragon, I felt like a good-for-nothing deadweight. And for years after my transformation, I convinced myself that those feelings I had about myself were caused by other people. That I was *misunderstood*."

I roll my eyes at myself.

"But I'm beginning to think that those fears we have about ourselves only really become true once *we* believe them. Other people might plant the seeds of insecurity, but we're the ones that water those fears until they're as tall as magic beanstalks shooting into the sky."

The Enchanted Bluebell

Looking over at Cam, I attempt to smile without bearing my fangs too much.

"So no, I don't think you're a coward or an incapable wizard. You're just afraid that you're those things."

Silence settles between us. A minute or so later, Cam is the one to speak again.

"I'm sorry that I snapped at you in the observatory. I really was concerned for your safety, but I was angry too. I was just starting to think that maybe I'd found an ally in this magical mess with the portal and the missing keys to the castle, only to have those hopes dashed when I realized that you weren't a real dragon."

My wings bob up and down as I shrug my shoulders. "Yeah well, you were kind of right to worry. If I'd been a real dragon, the bluebell's magic wouldn't have been able to transport me to…wherever this place is."

The Enchanted Bluebell

I look around the dark cavern wondering, not for the first time, where the enchanted bluebell has taken us.

Hm…

Now that I've stopped moving long enough to think instead of panic, the gears in my brain start to turn. Perhaps *where* is the wrong question. Maybe we should be asking *why*. When the bluebell's magic reached out to me, I'd been wishing that I was somewhere besides Bellerose Castle. Not only that, but Cam just admitted that he doesn't want to find a way out of this place yet. Could it be that our situation is only partially the bluebell's doing?

I don't know much about magical artifacts and how they function, but I have this little thought. As soon as it pops into my mind, that thought begins to grow.

What if the enchanted bluebell provides the magic, but the people who interact with it provide the

The Enchanted Bluebell

intention? The last thing I thought before being dragged out of the dungeon was a wish to be somewhere else. What if the bluebell also took Cam's desire to be isolated into consideration as well? I'm not sure how accurate my assumption is, but there's one way to put this theory to the test.

I scoot closer to Cam so I can look into his eyes. As calmly as I can, I say, "I know you don't feel ready to return to the castle, Cam, but we left the bluebell unguarded without even the glass case. So Tawny, Elliot, Josephine, and Sasha are all in danger. If we're trapped in this cavern, then we can't help them."

At the reminder, Cam's shoulders hunch, as if he's just recalled the weight upon them.

"You're right." He sighs and climbs to his feet. "They're all asleep. They have no idea what's happened in the dungeon." He brushes off his pajama pants and straightens his housecoat. "I might know a spell that can pinpoint our location. It'll take some trial and error, though."

"I can live with trial and error," I reply. "It's a step in the right direction."

No sooner does Cam close his eyes in concentration than I feel a pull in the air. Not unlike the pull that brought us here from the dungeon. I look around to see what—if anything—just happened, but without Cam's glowing eyes, the cavern is pitch black. A gentle nudge to his shoulder prompts him to open his eyes.

Silver light once again fills the cavern. On the other side of the pool, directly across from us, a door has been carved into the stone wall.

"I didn't do that," Cam tells me, sounding befuddled.

"I believe you."

The Enchanted Bluebell

It plays into my theory about the bluebell's magic. That door didn't appear until *both* of us decided that we wanted to go back to the castle.

The wizard and I have our own speedy means of reaching the door on the opposite shore: I can fly and Cam has his magic. For some reason—maybe the last bit of reluctance to return—Cam decides to walk to the door by treading on the rocky shoreline. And for some reason—possibly my own reluctance to take up my solitary, lonely existence again—I decide to walk with him.

The silence between us feels companionable, so I'm a little disappointed when Cam breaks it by saying, "I've only ever heard you say nice things."

The noise I make is somewhere between a scoff and a bark of laughter. "I've definitely said mean things, Cam. To you and about you."

A smile tugs at the corner of his mouth. "I meant every time I've heard you speak English.

The Enchanted Bluebell

You've only said nice and encouraging things, at least to begin with. And every time you get upset, you revert back to speaking dragon." He shrugs. "I could be wrong, but that seems significant."

I don't have much time to ponder what he means by that before we're standing in front of the door. Cam grips the long, curved handle and pushes the door open.

The Enchanted Bluebell

Chapter Fourteen

On the other side of the magic door is the sitting room full of Josephine's knitting and embroidery. The fireplace is cold and dark. The castle is quiet.

"Maybe we got back before anything calamitous happened," Cam whispers. He glances at me and then does a double take. "Um...Nina?"

"What?"

He blinks at me with silver eyes that no longer glow. "Had to be sure it was you. You, uh...look different."

"I do?"

Cam waves his hands over the ashes in the hearth and utters a spell. The scattered ashes bind together, becoming smoother and more reflective until they've transformed into a mirror. Cautiously, I shuffle over to stand beside Cam and peer down into the looking glass.

The room is only lit by a small, floating sphere that hovers near the ceiling. It is sufficient light to see my reflection, although I find myself more inclined to blame the light than to believe my eyes.

There, staring back at me in the glass, is the face of a woman. She looks like an old acquaintance, one I haven't seen in years and whose visage I barely recognize. Long red hair frames her face, and seafoam green eyes blink in stunned incredulity.

I don't fully realize that the woman is meant to be me until I raise one wingtip to touch the mirror and the woman copies my movement, resting one finger against the looking glass. I look between the mirror and my wing. Except it's not a wing—it's a human hand.

Oh! That's *me*.

The Enchanted Bluebell

Now that I take a second look, I can see definite traces of dragon in my human appearance. My skin bears a distinct scaly pattern, and while it was once the hue of buttermilk, it's now taken on more of the brown coloring I had as a dragon. My red hair is tangled in the curved black horns that still grace the sides of my head, and some of my teeth feel more like fangs when I prod at them with my tongue.

But the rest of me is entirely changed. My wings are gone, replaced by a pair of human arms and hands. My bulky lizard legs have become human ones that have no trouble walking. And my talons are now harmless, chubby toes.

The embarrassing sting of tears create heat and pressure around my eyes and nose.

I only remember that Cam is here when I feel him wrap something soft around my shoulders.

"Here. You may want to this."

The Enchanted Bluebell

Quickly, I wipe the back of my hand under my eyes, hoping he hasn't noticed the tears that escaped. I then realize two things simultaneously.

The first: I am naked. Not naked in the same way that I was as a dragon. Dragons have all their sensitive bits tucked away behind flaps of scaled armor. No, I'm currently naked in the human way. In the way that most humans don't want to be ninety percent of the time, where *everything* is out and on display.

The second: Cam has taken off his housecoat and draped it over my shoulders.

Gratefully, I slip my arms through the sleeves and pull the garment together in the front. I knot the ties securely at my waist. My cheeks are flaming when I turn to face Cam. He doesn't seem nearly as flustered by my sudden transformation and subsequent nudity, for which I'm thankful. Now that I'm covered, Cam eyes me up and down.

The Enchanted Bluebell

"I take it by your surprise that this is the first time you've ever transformed back into a human?" His gaze drifts to the horns poking out of my hair. "Well...mostly human."

"Yeah," I say breathlessly. I haven't heard my human voice in a decade. "This is a first."

"You look good." When he realizes what he's implied, Cam quickly backtracks. "Not that I looked! I mean, it was hard *not* to look. You were naked. I mean—"

"Cam," I interrupt his nervous rambling with a laugh. "I know what you meant." I take his hand. "Come on, let's go take care of that flower in the dungeon."

It's much easier to jog down the stone steps with human legs. I feel so much lighter, freer. It's such a delightful feeling that I don't notice that I'm still holding Cam's hand until we reach the bottom of the stairwell. By then I figure that I might as well

The Enchanted Bluebell

keep holding it as I pull him behind me toward the center of the dungeon where we left the enchanted bluebell. He doesn't seem to mind the contact since I feel his fingers give mine a squeeze.

The both of us halt when we reach the entryway. The glass box lays broken on the floor, shards of it glittering under the blue glow of the magical flower. The bluebell is hovering above its pedestal, seemingly innocuous—not that I'm fooled by appearances anymore.

"Well, we can't simply cover it up again," I note. "And it doesn't seem like a good idea to just leave it how it is."

"No, you're right," Cam agrees and rubs the back of his neck. "I might have something in my potion room that we can use to safely contain it. I'll go get it, and you stay here to guard the bluebell."

The Enchanted Bluebell

He tugs his hand out of mine and hurries toward the stairwell. He shouts back over his shoulder.

"Just don't touch it, Nina!"

I roll my eyes. "Thanks, I learned that lesson ten years ago!"

Satisfied by my response, Cam disappears up the stairs.

Left on my own, with nothing to do but wait for Cam's return, I stay at a safe distance and study the enchanted bluebell. It doesn't look any different now than it has in the past, so I don't think it was damaged when it zapped me and Cam elsewhere. Still feeling an unsettling cocktail of anxiety and the high from seeing my physical transformation, I find myself going through my normal routine I do when I check on the bluebell.

I walk the perimeter of the room and peer into empty cells.

The Enchanted Bluebell

Going through familiar motions soothes my frayed nerves a bit. But a worry in the back of my mind is starting to get louder, overpowering my initial elation upon seeing my reflection. What if this transformation is temporary? For all I know, I'll go to sleep tonight and wake up tomorrow a dragon once more. My first reaction to that thought is that I'll be crushed.

Will I be crushed, though? Wasn't I just beginning to find happiness here at Bellerose Castle even when I had the form of a dragon? I'll certainly be immensely disappointed if I revert to being a dragon in the future, but I think...I think I'll survive. I think I'll find happiness anyway.

Wrapped up in my tangle of thoughts, I don't immediately realize that one of the cells I've glanced into is, for once, *not* vacant.

I'm about to move on to the next cell when I pause and look again. My eyes meet the beady black eyes of a goblin crouched in the darkest corner. Very

The Enchanted Bluebell

rarely have I seen goblins in real life. The majority of people revile goblins almost as much as they hate dragons, so the race of short, green beings tends to keep to themselves and shun the rest of the world. Can't say I blame the goblin community.

I have nothing against goblins, but there are *zero* reasons that I should be seeing one in the dungeon of Bellerose Castle.

"Hey!" I'm used to hearing a baritone growl come out of my mouth when I snap at someone. My human voice isn't very intimidating. "What are you doing here?"

Instead of answering, the goblin lunges at me, running full tilt. Forgetting that I'm not a dragon anymore, I leap on him. With a hiss, the goblin rakes his razor-sharp nails across my exposed calf.

Crying out, I hop on one leg while clutching the other. Blood drips through my fingers.

The Enchanted Bluebell

"What I wouldn't give to still have talons," I mutter.

I hop and turn around to see the goblin leap at the enchanted bluebell. My heart jumps into my throat.

"Wait! Stop!"

It's too late. The moment the goblin's hands touch the flower's stem, there's a flash of blue light. The goblin vanishes in an explosion that rocks the dungeon walls. When the dust settles, there's no sign of the intruder. I don't know if he's dead or just transported somewhere else—with this flower, who knows?

Reluctantly, I let go of my bleeding wound and run as fast as I can for the stairs. I feel blood running down my leg, but even more concerning than that, I hear a commotion somewhere upstairs. It's not until I get to the top of the dungeon stairwell that I pinpoint where the noise is coming from.

The Enchanted Bluebell

It's coming from the bathroom on the second floor. Where the magic portal is.

Cam comes sprinting down the corridor toward me, wide-eyed and breathing hard. His silver eyes grow even bigger when he takes in the bloody gashes on my leg. "Nina, what's going on?"

I'm not entirely sure, but...

"I think the castle is under attack."

The Enchanted Bluebell

Chapter Fifteen

Cam and I rush up to the second floor, heading toward the clamor in the bathroom. A beam of gold light streams out of the cupboard beneath the sink. I raise a hand to shield my eyes. Not for the first time tonight, I wish that I was wearing more than a housecoat.

"Do you think that's where the goblin came from?" I shout over the roar emitted by the magical portal.

"What goblin?" Cam shouts back.

I don't have the chance to answer him.

A goblin is shot out of the magic portal like he was launched from a cannon. The small man gets slammed into the wall, cracking his skull on the stone. Cam surges forward and pulls the bathroom

The Enchanted Bluebell

door shut. That won't stop the invaders in the long run, but it might slow them down.

"We need to wake everyone up," Cam concludes, gasping breath. "Tell them to meet up in the War Room."

"Got it!" I pull away from him but turn back a second later. "Where is the War Room?"

After giving me brief directions—apparently, the War Room is an offshoot of the library—I run to Tawny's suite. In the past, I've been afraid to venture too far into her suite; she has so many bookshelves filled with alchemy textbooks and fragile glass bottles, I feared that I'd knock over entire shelves with one sweep of my tail. I still feel that jolt of nerves as I tear into her sitting room before I remember that I don't have a huge tail anymore.

I'm still not used to running on two legs and nearly trip over a coffee table. When I get to Tawny's bedroom, I tumble through the doorway.

The Enchanted Bluebell

Sprawled across her floor, I accidentally push over a pile of stacked books. At the noise, Tawny sits up in bed, ramrod straight.

"Who's there?!"

She grabs a large, hardcover tome from the bedside table and wields it above her head. Slowly, I stand up with my hands in the air and my head ducked in case she decides to hurl the book at me.

"It's me! It's Nina!"

Hesitantly, I raise my head to peek at her. Tawny turns on the lamp. She stares at me, opens her mouth but says nothing, and then continues to stare. Her brown eyes narrow—then widen and narrow again. She shakes her head. "No, no, no. Nina's a dragon. Who...who are you?"

"I *am* Nina," I insist. "Look!" I tilt my head toward her. "I still have the horns. And you can still see the pattern of my scales. See?" I push up the

The Enchanted Bluebell

sleeves of Cam's housecoat and angle my bare arms to catch the light from the lamp.

Tawny leans forward, staring at me in disbelief. She throws the blankets off and slides her legs over the side of her bed.

"Nina?"

"Yes!"

Upstairs, I hear the bathroom door get violently thrown open. Loud, angry voices come together in a war cry.

Tawny looks up at the ceiling. "What is that?"

"I don't have a lot of time to explain," I say, grabbing her hand. "Long story short, I'm not really a dragon. I've been under a spell. Also, there are goblins invading the castle. Come on, we have to hurry!"

The Enchanted Bluebell

We never make it to the War Room. The two of us end up running into Cam and Elliot in the corridor outside Tawny's suite. Sasha zips out of his bedroom, apparently needing nothing but the thunderous cacophony overhead to wake him.

"Leave Grandma," Elliot says when I make a move in the direction of Josephine's suite. "She's probably safer if she stays where she is."

Tawny lays a hand on the young shapeshifter's shoulder. "Will you stay with Grandma, Sasha?"

"What? But I can help!"

"You will be helping," she assures him. "This way, we'll know that Grandma has someone to protect her."

With a dramatic sigh, Sasha shifts into a brown dog and runs off to find Josephine.

"Now what?" asks Elliot.

The Enchanted Bluebell

"They're after the enchanted bluebell," I assert. "I caught one of the goblins in the dungeon attempting to steal it."

Tawny reaches out and takes my hand. "Nina and I will go downstairs to guard the bluebell. Cam, go upstairs with Elliot and close the portal."

I don't know who's more astounded that Cam doesn't hem and haw in order to stall. I guess I shouldn't count myself among those pleasantly surprised by the way he dashes to the stairwell with all the determination in the world since I was the one who gave him that pep talk. But go he does, with more confidence than I've ever seen from him, leaving a stunned Elliot to follow in his wake.

Tawny purses her lips. "Cam seems different..." Then she looks at me. "Did something happen before the goblin invasion?"

The Enchanted Bluebell

Smiling, I shrug. "Cam and I did some soul searching, that's all. Come on, let's go guard that flower."

***

Our new plan goes awry as soon as Tawny and I make it down to the dungeon. The glass case remains in pieces on the floor, and the goblin who attacked me is still gone, but so is the enchanted bluebell.

"Uh..." Tawny groans with anxiety. "Where is the bluebell? Did you move it, Nina?"

"No! It was right here just a minute ago!"

The two of us fan out to search the surrounding cells, but the bluebell is nowhere. Tawny's fingers flutter, apprehensively fluffing her hair. "Sooo, you're human now?" Tawny glances at me over her shoulder. "How did that happen? And why are you wearing Cam's bathrobe?"

"I don't know," I reply in answer to the first question. "I haven't had much time to contemplate the situation. As for Cam's housecoat, I never wore clothes as a dragon, so..."

"And the goblins..." Tawny trails off. Her dark eyes are wide, and her chest begins to rise and fall rapidly. I rush over to her, taking her by the shoulders.

"Tawny, breathe!"

"I can't!" she gasps. "We lost the enchanted bluebell! If anyone finds out..."

I shake her a little. "No one's going to find out, Tawny. We'll search the whole castle until we find it."

She nods and sucks in a few deep breaths. Once I'm convinced that she's not about to

The Enchanted Bluebell

hyperventilate, I take Tawny's hand and drag her with me as I run back up the stairs. "Cam!" I shout. "Elliot! We have a problem!"

I still hear the uproar from the second-floor bathroom; however, the soft glow of light coming from the sitting room catches my eye. It's brighter than the floating nightlight that I had used to see my reflection earlier. Is someone in there?

Tawny and I exchange cautious yet curious looks and creep closer.

Upon entering the room, I see that someone has turned on the lamp beside the wicker chair where Josephine likes to crochet and knit. I'm more than a little confused to see Josephine seated in her chair when last I knew, the retired fairy godmother had been asleep in her bed.

Josephine sits with her bony hands folded in her lap, looking rather annoyed but not distressed. Then I look down and see Sasha seated at

The Enchanted Bluebell

Josephine's feet. His angry expression is a thin veil for the spark of fear that I can see just behind the kid's eyes. He's glaring at the far corner. I turn to see what has incited his animosity, only to feel the tingle of magic in my extremities. Suddenly, my arms and legs refuse to obey me. They're frozen in place. I am able to crane my neck, though, to see who's just cast this spell.

A petite blonde woman wearing a midnight blue dress hovers in a dark corner. Underneath the chaotic noises coming from upstairs, I hear the hum of dainty wings beating. Tawny sounds devastated when she whispers, "Ella? Is that you?"

Ella. The fairy godmother who kicked me out of the boutique. The woman smiles cruelly.

"Have a seat, you two."

Her voice is cheerful, but it does nothing to warm my cold legs as they move without my consent.

The Enchanted Bluebell

Tawny and I walk like robots to join Sasha on the floor. Ella claps her hands.

"Well, now it's a party! I'm sure Elliot and that incompetent wizard of yours will join us soon. But in the meantime, who wants to help me with this?"

She flies to the side, revealing another goblin standing behind her. There's something wrong with this one, though. It looks like he's been transformed into a stone statue. And clutched in his hand is the enchanted bluebell.

The Enchanted Bluebell

Chapter Sixteen

Ella the fairy godmother clenches one hand in a fist. Then she pulls her arm back and swings it, spreading her fingers viciously in the direction of the goblin turned to stone. The poor goblin's arm explodes in a spray of gray rock, and the enchanted bluebell floats gracefully to the floor. There it lays, deceptively innocuous.

"Now which one of you knows how to temporarily neutralize this flower?" she asks.

All of us remain silent—me because I genuinely have no idea. My eyes dart to the right. Tawny just looks scared and confused. To my left, Sasha is still masking his own fear with audacious anger. The only one here who might know what Ella is talking about is—

"Josephine!" A menacing smile appears on Ella's face as she flies closer. "This seems like it

The Enchanted Bluebell

would be in your wheelhouse. Or perhaps your dragon will know what to do. Where is the beast?"

Rather than give her an answer, Josephine shakes her head with a *tsk*. "Oh, Ella. You've always looked for the easiest path to success. That's why you've never made it farther than the boutique."

The blonde sneers at Josephine.

"Is that what you think I'm doing? Let me tell you, it hasn't been *easy* trying to open a portal inside Bellerose Castle. No, I'm merely righting a wrong done to our community years ago. As soon as it became clear how dangerous the enchanted bluebell truly was, it should have been handed over to the Fairy Godmother Counsel. After all, we deal with enchantments all the time, especially enchanted flowers. But no, the governor entrusted the bluebell to *you* specifically. And all you did was stow it away in your basement when you should have been studying it and figuring out how to utilize its magical properties!"

The Enchanted Bluebell

Josephine's expression softens slightly. "I'm sorry you feel that you and the Counsel were snubbed, Ella. But it's becoming quite clear to me that you would have run afoul of this flower in your pursuit to profit from it."

"And what's becoming clear to *me* is how we have allowed your boundless arrogance to go unchecked for decades."

Ella's cheeks burn red when Josephine chuckles at her.

"It's not arrogance, dear. I just have a healthy respect for things that I don't yet understand. The enchanted bluebell, for example." Josephine tips her head toward the flower. "I've had a theory about its magic for quite some time, but I had to be patient and wait for a key piece of evidence to come along."

Ella's nose wrinkles. "You don't mean that clumsy dragon, do you?"

The Enchanted Bluebell

"Indeed, I do." Josephine's smile brightens. "The last time a dragon ventured this far into the city, it was ten years ago. It was that small dragon that attacked the governor's palace."

All the blood drains from my head. It's a good thing I'm already seated on the floor, otherwise I might have fallen flat on my face in shock. She's talking about *me*. I'm the dragon that attacked the palace a decade ago—except I didn't attack anyone! When I awoke after touching the bluebell, the governor's security detail rushed me with their weapons drawn. I was terrified and discombobulated. All I did was run away from them.

"The theory has always been that the dragon was attempting to steal the enchanted bluebell," Josephine continues. "However, accounts of that day have never explained how the dragon got inside the palace without being seen. It's as if the creature materialized out of thin air. I don't believe that's really what happened, though. I think someone in attendance at the exhibit got a little too close to the bluebell and fell victim to an accidental enchantment. Not unlike your goblin friend over there."

Josephine points one knobby finger at the stone goblin across the room. Radiating skepticism, Ella looks between the goblin statue and Josephine.

"Why would the bluebell transform someone into a dragon, of all things?"

My heart pounds against my ribs as I peer up at Josephine from under my lashes. The old woman's smile now has a twinge of sorrow to it.

"Because that's how the poor girl thought of herself. And I'm sure that the way people treated her *after* she looked like a dragon did nothing to dispel the enchantment."

I try to swallow, but my mouth has gone bone dry. Josephine's warm gaze briefly meets mine.

The Enchanted Bluebell

"It wasn't until our dear dragon began to show others the grace she wished to be shown—began to show kindness to those who were unkind—that the spell began to unravel." The retired fairy godmother gives Ella a look of pity. "I can only imagine what you might turn into should you wander too close to that flower, Ella."

The blonde fairy scoffs.

"I won't have to touch that thing as soon as the rest of those filthy goblins get through the portal."

"Hey!" Sasha jumps to his feet, eyes blazing with fury. "They're not filthy, they're people!"

Rolling her eyes, Ella flicks a finger at Sasha. A shower of white sparks swirls around him, and he's forced down to the floor again. "Be quiet, hon. The adults are talking."

"You think your minions will be any help?" Tawny spits at Ella. She's over her initial shock.

The Enchanted Bluebell

Now anger and betrayal are coming to the forefront. "Look what happened to *him*."

She nods to the stone statue.

"And the goblin I saw in the dungeon got zapped out of the castle entirely as soon as he touched the flower," I add.

Instantly, I regret opening my mouth. Ella's cold eyes snap to me, narrowing to slits. "Who are you?" She takes in the horns on my head, and a grin slowly creeps across her face. "Wait...don't tell me that *you're* the dragon."

I clench my jaw and say nothing, but I guess the silence in the room is the only confirmation Ella needs. She snaps her fingers and beckons me forward.

"Excellent. Come over here."

For a second, I consider defying her just on principle. Ella has already demonstrated that she can

The Enchanted Bluebell

control my movements, though. If I don't stand up and start walking, she can just use her magic to force me, which wasn't so pleasant the first time I experienced it. So, against my better judgment, I willingly get to my feet and approach her.

The floor is cold under my bare feet, but it gradually warms the closer I get to the enchanted bluebell. There's a soft blue glow around the flower's petals. Despite the eventful night it's had, the bluebell doesn't appear damaged.

I halt once I'm standing in front of Ella and the flower. She's such a tiny woman that I would tower over her, except her gossamer wings lift her higher in the air so the two of us are at eye level. Ella's cerulean eyes are beautiful but shallow; as if there's a layer of ice just beneath the surface. She points down to the flower that lays between us.

"Since you've already gone one round with the enchanted bluebell, let's see who wins round two."

The Enchanted Bluebell

Fear is quick to fill me. I haven't been human again for even an hour, and already my time as a hominid might be at an end. I close my eyes, inhaling harshly through my nose. I remind myself that I've considered the possibility that my transformation may not be permanent. But I was well on my way to finding peace as a dragon; I don't need to be human to have a good life.

My eyes pop open when Ella snaps her fingers in front of my face. "Pay attention," she chides me. Then she gestures to the flower on the floor. "Don't pick it up. I just want you to touch the stem."

Dread pools in my belly as I bend down. I swallow hard, trying not to be sick. I don't know if the magical flower has sentience, but if it does, it probably won't appreciate being covered in vomit.

With a trembling hand, I reach out and graze one fingertip over the bluebell's green stem.

The Enchanted Bluebell

Chapter Seventeen

Warmth spreads from the point of contact between me and the bluebell and then travels up my arm. I wince, bracing myself for the re-emergence of scales, fangs, and wings. I can live with being a dragon. The important part is that I save everyone else from Ella and the goblins. And if being a dragon makes that possible, then who am I to dread that?

No transformation happens, though. Instead, a blue glow climbs up my arm, leaving a soothing tingle in its wake. A voice that is somehow both strange and familiar whispers in my ear.

Why are you afraid?

I glance up at Ella. She stands a cautious distance away, watching me. I don't say anything in response to the question—no one else seems to have heard it—but I get the impression that the voice has its answer.

The Enchanted Bluebell

Just like earlier in the night, a ribbon of blue energy slithers out of the bluebell's mouth. But rather than go after *me* again, it strikes out at Ella. Half a scream comes out of her mouth before the ribbon of energy swirls around her and mutes her voice. Then there's a brilliant flash of blue that forces me to shield my eyes.

My eyes blink behind the safety of my hands. After a second, it appears as though the bright light has vanished, but I peek between my fingers just in case. Black spots invade my vision; however, I can see well enough to ascertain that Ella is no longer in the sitting room.

"What was that?" Tawny gasps. She rubs at her eyes.

"That was awesome!" Sasha jumps to his feet, pumping his fist in the air.

Josephine pushes herself out of the armchair and extends a finger to the nearby lampshade.

The Enchanted Bluebell

"Would you look at this?" A fond smile graces her face as she picks up a blue butterfly on her finger. "You do make a pretty butterfly, Ella. I'd say you got off easy, all things considered." The old woman's gaze then cuts to me. "It looks like you won round two, Nina."

"I'm not so sure about that," I confess. "It didn't feel like a fight. It felt more like...teamwork."

Tawny comes forward for a closer look at Ella the butterfly. "What are we going to do with her?"

"For now, we should take her up to my greenhouse," her grandmother suggests.

As if to remind all of us that there's still an ongoing crisis, a particularly loud explosion from the upstairs bathroom booms and echoes through the halls of the castle. My eyes widen. Cam! I completely forgot about him. Tawny and I look at

The Enchanted Bluebell

each other over the top of Sasha's head, wearing twin expressions of horror.

"The portal," I say, feeling a pit of trepidation form in my stomach.

"Elliot!"

Tawny takes off running for the stairs. Sasha shifts into a raven and flies over our heads while I bring up the rear.

I follow the frantic bounce of Tawny's black curls. In the back of my mind, I wonder how we're going to help Cam and Elliot when none of us are armed, nor do we know how to close the magic portal. But we can't just abandon them, so we'll have to come up with something.

As we sprint down the hallway toward the bathroom, I notice that the walls appear to be melting. The stonework looks like gooey candlewax. The glowing orbs that usually provide light in the dark corridors have turned into glowing sunflower heads, and the portraits and paintings that hang from the walls are now funhouse mirrors and window boxes full of hissing flowers that snap their fangs at us as we pass.

The boys are just outside the bathroom door. Cam has created some kind of force field to stop the goblins—who are in full battle armor—from advancing farther down the hallway. One of them manages to slip past Cam's spell-work only to face Elliot, who's wielding an upturned coat rack. He swings the pole and clocks the goblin across the jaw, sending him down to the floor where the goblin wisely stays.

It would be a humorous sight to see the two men clad in their pajamas battling goblins, except that I'm no better off, rushing into the fight wearing nothing but a housecoat.

"We can't keep this up, Cam!" Elliot shouts.

The Enchanted Bluebell

Sasha swoops down, shifting into a small lion. His roar reverberates along the stone walls. Startled, the goblins actually retreat for a minute. They're trapped, though, between the residents of Bellerose Castle and the magic portal in the bathroom. The portal looks and sounds unstable as it intermittently spits out fireworks and belches black smoke.

I clench my hands into fists and feel something clutched in my right hand. Looking down, I'm somewhat surprised to see that I'm holding the enchanted bluebell. I don't recall picking it up off the floor, but here it is. I peel my fingers back so that the flower is merely resting in the palm of my hand.

"This is my home," I whisper to the bluebell. "These are my friends."

Not that I want the goblins to get hurt; I just don't want them in the castle. I feel a warm pulse come from the flower in response. Its magical blue glow intensifies to the point where I have to squint and avert my gaze. Only at the last second do I think to yell a warning.

"Cam, Elliot! Get down!"

It's too bright for me to see if they've heard me.

This time, instead of one blue energy ribbon, a dozen shoot from the bluebell. They shatter Cam's force field and encircle the small army of goblins. It balls them up like they're caught in a big blue net and drags them back to the portal under the sink. The goblins' screams sound more frightened than pained. I hope the portal doesn't tear them to shreds, but it *is* the risk they accepted when they teamed up with Ella and her machinations.

The blue light and the pulsating warmth only recede when the goblins have been shoved through the portal and the cupboard door has slammed shut.

Silence, but for our labored breathing, falls over the corridor. As the effects of adrenaline wane,

The Enchanted Bluebell

exhaustion tightens its grip on me. My arms start to tremble with the effort of holding them up. I close my fingers over the bluebell's stem and allow my arms to drop to my sides.

With the portal closed, the hallway has reverted to its former state. I step forward on shaky legs to peek into the bathroom.

It's seen better days. The toilet bowl has been busted up even more, rendering it basically useless. The sink has a crack bisecting it, and the wall opposite is dented and scorched black. Besides the damage, the room actually looks like a bathroom. It's not a jungle or the inside of a geode.

I bend down to open the cupboard door. The only things under the sink are a toilet plunger and cleaning supplies. No signs of a magic portal.

Suddenly, the bluebell burns white hot in my grasp. I whirl around just as an errant goblin leaps at me with a desperate cry. Tawny and Elliot shout my

The Enchanted Bluebell

name, and Sasha the lion springs to my defense, but they're all too far away to be of much help. All I have time to do is cover my head.

The goblin's cry is abruptly cut off with a strangled gurgle.

With a spurt of green blood, the tip of a sword emerges from the goblin's throat. *Shing* goes the sword as it's drawn back. The goblin collapses revealing Cam, in his flannel pajamas, holding the bloodied sword. My heart pounds, and I struggle to catch my breath.

"Where did *that* come from?" I gasp.

Chest heaving, Cam lowers the sword. "Hidden pocket," he answers and pats his pajama top.

The danger finally seems to have passed when Sasha shifts back into a boy. Everyone slumps forward and wearily leans against the walls, though their eyes remain alert just in case the fight isn't

The Enchanted Bluebell

really over. My eyes meet Cam's. I don't quite know how to thank him for what he just did. A grateful nod is all I can manage. I guess it's enough since he nods back.

"So..." Elliot puts down the coat rack. "Who wants breakfast?"

The Enchanted Bluebell

Chapter Eighteen

Looking in the mirror, I smooth out the wrinkles in my rustic-orange dress and toy with the embroidered flowers and orange slices on the bodice. The full-length mirror leans against my bedroom wall—the same bedroom I had back when I was a dragon. The only thing I've changed about it is the futon mattresses; soon after I became human again, I decided it was time to upgrade to a real bed. Well, I suppose I have made one other change besides the bed. Cam and Josephine worked together to shape some of the castle's liminal space into a walk-in closet while Tawny took me shopping for clothes.

It's been two months since I became human once more, and so far, the change seems to be permanent. Some of my dragon features continue to linger, like the horns as well as the color and the scaly

The Enchanted Bluebell

pattern of my skin. I'm getting used to my new appearance, but I don't think I look all that bad.

Satisfied with my new dress, I bend down to lace my boots and then exit my room.

Right outside my bedroom, Josephine's greenhouse is filled with butterflies of all kinds. Ella has remained with us here in Bellerose Castle. In her butterfly form, she would be in danger of being eaten by birds out in the wild—especially since it seems that she can't use her magic anymore. I'm amazed by Josephine's goodwill toward the treacherous fairy godmother. She has gone out of her way to make Ella feel at home in the greenhouse, even going so far as to provide other butterflies for Ella's company.

I wave good morning to the fluttering insects as I pass through the room on my way to the stairwell.

I smell bacon and onions cooking long before I reach the kitchen.

The Enchanted Bluebell

Elliot stands by the stovetop, flipping bacon strips in one pan while he scrambles eggs for omelets in another. At the other end of the stove, Cam lifts a whistling kettle to pour hot water into a teacup.

"How nice is it to have running water again?" says Elliot with a giant smile on his face.

Tawny chuckles as she delivers a platter of fruit to the table. "You've been saying that every day for the past two weeks."

"And I still feel like shouting it from the rooftops." Elliot giddily turns on the tap to wash his hands.

It'd taken a while to get a new water tank installed in the castle. Elliot has been the one who struggled the most, so it's hard to begrudge him his enthusiasm. Besides, he isn't wrong. It *is* nice to have running water again. It hasn't been enjoyable walking to the nearest convenience store to buy enough water for six people's daily use.

The Enchanted Bluebell

"I thought it was fun when the castle was flooded," Sasha chimes in. "I hardly ever get to go swimming."

"Perhaps that will be the next renovation that Cam and I tackle," Josephine says. "We can put a pool in the dungeon now that it's no longer being used."

It's true—the enchanted bluebell no longer sits in a glass box in the dungeon. After our battle with Ella and the goblins, I got the feeling that the magical flower didn't appreciate being down in that cold, dark place all alone every day. So, Cam crafted a special vase for the bluebell to safely rest in, and each day, we place the vase in a different room of the castle. Today, the flower is joining us for meals in the kitchen. It sits on a shelf above the sink right in front of the window that looks out on a cobblestone courtyard.

I walk up to the counter, behind Sasha, to grab a plate and silverware. "Good morning, Nina!"

The Enchanted Bluebell

the boy says before rushing off to get his share of the bacon.

"Good morning," I reply to his retreating back.

Sasha's cheerful greeting never fails to put me in a good mood. How did I go for so many years without anyone bidding me good morning the way that kid does?

I take my plate to my spot at the table where I find a cup of steaming black tea already waiting for me. Cam sits in his chair, sipping his own tea and reading a book from the library.

"Thank you," I tell him as I pull out my chair and sit.

"For what?" he asks and innocently flips a page.

I roll my eyes. "Oh, you know." I reach over and pinch his arm.

The Enchanted Bluebell

"Ow!"

Cam dramatically drops the book in his lap. He rubs his arm and raises his head, prepared to tell me off. He catches sight of my appearance, though, and his mouth just hangs open. Whatever response he'd been ready to deliver evidently dies on his tongue. I sit up a little straighter in my chair and smooth out my dress again.

"Well...what do you think?"

His silver eyes sweep down the length of me—what he can see, anyway—and then dart back up to my face. "What?"

"The dress. You don't think it's too much?"

"No," he replies quickly. "No, it's a special day. That calls for a special outfit. I think you look nice. Very nice."

A pleasant heat rises to my cheeks. "Thanks. You don't look so bad yourself."

The Enchanted Bluebell

Today, he's wearing black trousers, a white shirt, and a dark purple vest. Ever since that eventful night, I've noticed that Cam hasn't attended breakfast in his pajamas and housecoat. Instead, he always comes to the table freshly showered and neatly dressed. He still reads while he drinks his tea, of course, but he doesn't get quite so lost in the pages lately, paying more attention to the people around him.

At my compliment, I notice that he does the same thing I did a moment ago: straightens his posture and searches for wrinkles in his shirt that need eradicating.

"It's a good thing," I continue with a knowing grin, "since you're coming with me."

Cam inhales too fast and chokes, presumably on his own saliva since there's nothing in his mouth. "Nina, you're reuniting with your family for the first time in a decade."

The Enchanted Bluebell

As if I could forget.

"Do you really want me there to meet them?"

I hunch my shoulders a bit. It hadn't occurred to me that Cam might not feel comfortable going with me. I probably should have run it by him first before assuming anything. But now it's out in the open, and I'm not sure how to retract it.

"Well, I'll be even more nervous than I already am if I go alone," I confess.

He nods, contemplating his plate before looking up to meet my gaze again. "As long as you're sure, then I'm there."

His words imbue me with a sense of calm. Impulsively, I place my hand over his.

"All right, you two," Elliot interjects, carrying a pan of bacon over to the table. "Stop flirting and dish up."

The Enchanted Bluebell

Our hands hurriedly separate to make room for the hot pan.

Breakfast goes by in a rush. Throughout the meal, I'm conscious of my napkin placement. It won't be the end of the world to meet my family with a syrup stain on the front of my dress, but it wouldn't be a great first impression either. It might be my imagination, but it looks like Cam is also being more careful while he eats now that he's agreed to accompany me.

As soon as he's finished, Cam stands up and starts collecting empty plates, taking them to the sink with an air of nervousness. Wiping my sweaty palms on my dress, I rise from my chair too, ready to leave and get this over with. However, Tawny intercepts me before I can escape the kitchen.

She's dressed in a very similar outfit as she was the day we first met: a pair of jeans and her soft-looking navy-blue jacket. Her wild curls are held back by a gold cloth headband, bringing out tiny

The Enchanted Bluebell

flecks of gold in her brown eyes. Those eyes have a kindhearted twinkle in them.

"I know you have somewhere to be," she says, "but I just wanted to tell you something before you left."

Tawny reaches out and takes my hands.

"No matter how today goes, I want you to know that I am *so* glad I sprung you from that Creature Control shelter."

Using our clasped hands, I pull her into a hug. My throat feels tight, so my words come out sort of hoarse.

"Thank you for finding me."

Tawny draws back, her eyes glassy. "Go get 'em, dragon lady."

Leaving the kitchen, I wait at the door to Rose Red Courtyard. It's several minutes later when I'm finally joined by the castle's resident wizard. He

The Enchanted Bluebell

looks just as anxious as I feel, if that's possible. Wanting to break the tension, and maybe give him a different reason to be preoccupied, I lean forward and plant a kiss on the corner of his mouth. Cam's eyebrows shoot up almost to his hairline.

"What was that for?"

"For luck." I link my fingers with his. "And because I wanted to."

I lift my free hand to grab the brand-new key to Bellerose Castle. It hangs from a hook on the wall near the red door. The key is another product of Cam and Josephine's recent teamwork. As I grasp the handle, I hear Cam clear his throat.

"Will you be requiring more good luck before we meet up with your family?"

"Oh, you can never have enough good luck," I tell him quite seriously.

The Enchanted Bluebell

Feeling Cam squeeze my hand, I pull the door open. The sun shines down on the bustling courtyard, lighting the world with tranquil, golden beams. Hand in hand, Cam and I step outside and close the door to Bellerose Castle behind us.

The End

Acknowledgments

All the thanks in the world go to Erin Lee, the editors, and everyone else at Crazy Ink. It's been my dream to be a published author ever since I was a teenager, and you guys have all helped make that dream come true.

Thank you to my parents, who have been nothing but supportive. And thanks to the rest of my friends and family. You guys are my biggest fans, buying my books and spreading the word about me.

The Enchanted Bluebell

About the Author

Traumatized as a child by the haunted house at the Minnesota State Fair, McKenzie Rae decided to take that fear and use it to write as many twisted, spooky, and mysterious tales as she could think of. As a result, she is still afraid of the dark, and some nights, she is convinced that a monster is under her bed. But that could just be her cat.

Rae is still trying to figure out how the real world works, so she creates fantasy worlds where anything can happen. The *Dysfunctional* trilogy were the first three books she ever published. Since then, she has written chilling tales such as *My Dark Passenger*, *Now That I'm Alone*, and *The Dark Fae Series*, just to name a few.

With every book she writes, Rae brings the dark worlds in her imagination to life, and she invites all of you to explore them with her.

The Enchanted Bluebell

Follow McKenzie Rae

Website: https://mckenzierswenson.wixsite.com/website

Facebook: https://www.facebook.com/authormckenzierae/

Instagram: https://www.instagram.com/kenzi707rae/

Goodreads: https://www.goodreads.com/author/show/17380566.McKenzie_Rae

Pinterest: https://www.pinterest.com/kenzi707/pins/

***

Other Books by McKenzie Rae

Dysfunctional: Series

My Dark Passenger (Missy's Story #1)

Now That I'm Alone (Missy's Story #2)

All that Remains (Missy's Story #3)

The Rain Came Down

The Enchanted Bluebell

The Back of Beyond

Between Wind and Water: A Creature Feature Series Novella

Changeling (Book One of the Dark Fae Series)

Faery Tales (Book Two of the Dark Fae Series)

The Enchanted Bluebell

CRAZY
INK

Copyright © 2022 by Crazy Ink

All rights reserved. No part of this publication may be reproduced, distributed or transmitted in any form or by any means, without prior written permission.

Publisher's Note: This is a work of fiction. Names, characters, places, and incidents are a product of the author's imagination. Locales and public names are sometimes used for atmospheric purposes. Any resemblance to actual people, living or dead, or to businesses, companies, events, institutions, or locales is completely coincidental.

Made in the USA
Monee, IL
03 January 2022